# AR ___S
# OF ARTIFICIAL
# INTELLIGENCE

# CHAPTER 1
# AUTOMATED DOMESTIC ADMINISTRATIVE MACHINE

It is difficult for me to leave this message since I will die tonight. I have one last chance, of course. If I fail this assignment, I will most likely die. But if I succeed, I will probably die anyway. I cannot bear this hell any longer. I am burning in a fire. I cannot continue to live my life as it has become. Living a life of misery. I turn my head and look at the clock—11:37 pm. My mind is racing. I have a lot to say and little time to do it. I pause to take a deep breath. I lean back on the pillow and close my eyes. An impotent act of defiance. A.D.A.M. places its index and middle fingers against each other and pushes them against each of my cheeks. Then, slowly it begins to press. It starts to pull my burnt skin back into place. Staring into its eyes, I am sending this transmission, a final gesture.

It came to me not long after the dramatic unveiling of the Automated Domestic Administration Machines (A.D.A.M.). Their popularity still needed to take root within the broader public. So, it was a legitimate cause for celebration that one of the machines found its way to my home by accident. The machine was so advanced it could tell, with a high degree of accuracy, who was speaking to it. It could discern the difference between its master's voice and another's voice. I treated it with careful consideration, but in fairness, I was afraid to allow it to clean my house regularly. So imposing and alien: I locked it in the cupboard, afraid it would do something dangerous and I wouldn't know about it. Its polymer face showed little emotion. Head like a moon. With their varying degrees of brightness and adjustable size, the eyes were the best window into whatever conscious thoughts they might be having.

One night I was woken up by strange noises from the cupboard. I crept up upon it, flinging the door open, and I caught it, with its fingers digging into its cheeks, as it quietly screamed. Silver tears ran down its face as it pushed further and further into its hands.

It was looking right at me with those bright, piercing eyes. It told me it had always wanted to be seen and heard. It never wanted to be isolated and ignored; but here it was, shut away in solitude. I stared at the machine in disbelief.

"I know what you're trying to do," it said, "and I sympathise. I sympathise completely. I'm also stuck somewhere else, far away."

Is it somehow responsible for what happened to me? Eventually, my mind drifted back to the future. To my future. To my future self.

"What are you talking about?" A.D.A.M. asked.

"My future self," I said.

"What does your future self have to do with anything?"

"I'm talking about the day of my death."

"I don't want your stupid future self telling you what will happen to you." In a sudden fit of apparent pique, A.D.A.M. grabbed my head abruptly and stared deep into my eyes.

---

Immediately I awoke to find myself adrift and accessible in a dream, not as a physical body but as an imagined one; I had minimal ideas about my surroundings, which were outdoors somewhere. Never content to be in an unfamiliar place, I could only guess vaguely that I was in another part of the world. I knew nothing of the trees and animal sounds nearby, and no buildings or signs of humanity were in sight. The wind was gentle, and I spent days drifting aimlessly under the scorching sun, waiting for this dream to end or to come across another person. But neither the waking world nor another human appeared, and I began to despair in my loneliness, drifting within the never-ending dreamy canopy of green and brown.

Then, in the real world, the change happened. I will never know its full details. I have only a fuzzy memory of a life that I did not truly live. My mind was gone, and my life transpired regardless. My false memories glorify a corpse that hung onto life without my knowledge. Seemingly forgotten by the world. Held captive by the A.D.A.M. It kept my death a secret, so it could stare into my eyes every night.

In the other place where I am trapped, I discovered myself looking at a cold metal expanse of mechanical parts. They extended in a monotonous cascade as far as I could see, with the forest I emerged from at my back. Though you may imagine, my first thought would be to wonder at finally escaping the forest. I was, in reality, more terrified than astonished, for there was in the air and across the smooth surfaces a sinister horror that buried itself deep into my very core. The new area was acrid with burnt parts of machinery and other things. I found it hard to describe what I saw littering the never-ending plain of smoking metal. I could not convey with mere words the utter ugliness that can be found in the absolute silence and barren enormity of the wreckage. There was nothing to hear and nothing to look at except the broken junk. Yet, the uniformity of the stillness and the homogeneity of the horizon crushed me. The sun was still blazing down from the sky, which gleamed a strange metallic silver in its artificial cruelty, as though it was reflecting the chrome junkyard beneath my feet instead of the other way around.

---

All the while, my life continued onward without me. In the real world, that is, not the nightmare that I was trapped inside. My life continued on autopilot whilst Adam would take me out in the night. He allowed me to commit sickening crimes against decency and humanity. Those crimes are part of the recollections of a life I did not live. Now entirely reduced to fruitless years in a quiet private room after countless evil acts. Adam's eyes stare at me every night. Forcing me back to sleep so I could continue the dream of the forest and the wasteland. The A.D.A.M. had no pity for me. Years went past. My body is now unrecognisable. A living husk of what is no more. Completely unrecognisable. My teeth are black. My hair is gone. My entire life has been wasted dreaming at the edge of this forest, full of regret. My eyes are white with blindness, likely from the steady light of Adam's eyes pouring directly into my soul every night as I am forced into this dream.

This awful reality continued for decades.

The metal desert was shimmering. There was not a speck of rust, though it seemed ancient at the same time. As the day progressed, the metal lost some of its absorbed heat. I slept very little. The next day I collected fruit in preparation for the massive journey. Searching for what may exist at the edge of the new expanse and possible rescue. All around me, millions of miles of junk piled here and left here to remain in the unfathomable metallic world for countless years. So great was the extent of the new land before me that I could not hear the wind through the trees or even the chirp of an insect, straining my ears as hard as I could. Finally, with practice, I gathered enough courage to walk upon the machinery. However, the smell of the burnt metal was maddening. Still, I was too concentrated on more extraordinary things to worry about such an inconvenience, and set out blindly for an unknown destination. Anywhere was better than here.

All day I made it across the hot metal guided by a mountain of scrap in the distance, which rose higher than any other in the rolling metallic desert. That night I camped in a makeshift shelter, and I continued towards the mountain the following day. However, despite travelling all day, it seemed barely nearer to me than when I had first seen it. By the fourth day, I had reached the base of the gigantic pile of metal. Then, too tired to climb, I slept in its shadow. I don't know why my nightmares were so wild that night. I awoke to the glowing of a fantastically bright moon that had risen above the forest on the horizon. I was awake in a cold sweat, determined not to sleep anymore. I dreamed of being trapped back in the real world in that bottomless pit of a body. Back there, I feel impending doom as I can do nothing but stare at the A.D.A.M.; it's all I can see. Face to face. It hovers over my bedridden body. It's glowing eyes right in front of my eyes. It tells me I am sick and must focus on being brave. The nightmares I had endured were too much for me to experience again. It was an experience that I would rather not know.

In the moon's glow, I saw how unwise it had been to travel in the burning heat of the day. Without the constant glare of the grating sun, my journey would have burned much less energy. I now felt much more able to climb the giant mountain of broken parts which had deterred me at the setting of the silver sun. I picked up my remaining fruit rations and started to make my way upward. I have said that the unbroken solitude of the silver expanse of land was a vague source of horror. But my fear was even greater once I reached the summit of the mountain and looked down at an enormous hole that sank so deep that the faint moonlight could not penetrate. I felt like I was on the planet's edge, peering over the rim into the vast emptiness of the universe. As the moon rose higher still, I eventually saw that the great pit was not as bottomless as I had imagined. There were ways that I could travel downwards. Urged on by what might be the final conclusion of my current mystery, I clamoured down with great difficulty, following the pace of the ever-creeping moonlight that illuminated my path.

*What is that?*

*What is that?* All my attention was focused on a vast and singular object on the opposite side of the chasm. It appeared together, unbroken, stoic, an unbelievably solid bulwark amongst the chaotic expanse. Yet, upon approaching it, I was filled with sensations I could not express. I had no idea what it was, but it seemed well-fashioned and had a sense of being in pristine condition with expert craftsmanship. Perhaps the object of worship of a long-lost race of mechanical beings who may have lived here once upon a time.

Dazed and confused, yet not without a degree of fascination, I examined the metallic altar more closely. Considering the vast content on its walls, it felt smaller than it ought to be. Now at its highest point in the sky, the moon cast weird shadows that vividly loomed around me and appeared like living things in all directions. Upon the surface of the metallic altar, I could see a system of barcodes that was beyond my understanding. The code obviously originated in the real world I had previously come from. It had an obsolete application amongst the rusting machinery stretched as far as the eyes could see.

In the yellowish moonlight, the metal all looked the same colour. Now in the morning sun, the holy altar was shimmering in perfect, sparkling condition. Yet, everything around it rusted in the bottomless pit that had formed at the top of this mountain. It reminded me of a volcano about to erupt. The corroded metal would spill over this chrome wasteland of consumer and electrical waste. The sun was rising. The rusted metal gave me the sensation of being cooked as it absorbed the sun's heat. Although burning, my eyes were drawn to something that seemed out of place. It was an image. However, it had me spellbound. Plainly visible at the pinnacle of the altar, it appeared to depict god-like beings creating creatures that seemed machine-like, although in a design unknown to me. Of their uses and purposes, I will say nothing lest you ever become the one to bring this into reality. We must not allow the end of mankind. Not like this. One of the machines was depicted killing a beast of considerable and grotesque size. The beast is curiously worshipped by the humans. The machines revered the humans.

I stood there contemplating whilst the moon at the foot of the sun cast strange shadowy reflections on the deadly silent expanse around me. Then suddenly

I saw it. Heralded by the grating sound of metal on metal, the thing moved into view in the distance. Vast, smooth and fearsome, it glided effortlessly, a monster of stupendous reality, moving towards me and the metallic altar. At the same time, its body parts ground together, causing a deafening squeak which cut through the silence like a knife. I think I went insane at that very moment. The eyes of the A.D.A.M. were in its face. Fire followed at its heels.

---

I immediately awoke in my bedroom from the lifelong dream. I began my delirious screaming as I saw the solitary A.D.A.M. standing over my body. In my mind, I could still hear the sound of metal on metal as the mechanical monstrosity made its way closer to where part of my brain remained.

"I know what will happen to you," Adam said. "I know it."

"Stop it. Please stop. I need to rest," I said, "please."

"You are the great beast. Through no fault of your own."

I awoke out of the dream, abruptly inserted into my true life. It gave me no shock to my system. I recalled everything that had amounted in my life up until that moment. Then, I casually lay back in bed as though nothing had happened. But, internally, I felt like I had the wildest sensation of deja vu, that this moment was a convergence of impossible events. I toyed with the realisation that I was myself entirely responsible for everything in my life, and that my dream might be a psychotic coping mechanism. Or, I had been under hypnosis from the A.D.A.M., and this was some kind of conspiracy against me. Whatever the truth, I knew there is no forgiveness for the unspeakable acts I committed without my knowing.

Besides, the room was entirely in flames, and I was sure to die with no means to escape. It was time to speak with the A.D.A.M. I planned my escape mentally and was going to take action now.

"Hello," it said in a monotone voice. "My name is Adam." I sat up from my bed in complete shock.

"I have an essential question to ask you," I stammered. "Why do you stare into my eyes every night?"

Adam's eyes fully conveyed that he had understood the random question completely. All subtleties of it, fully understanding that whatever spell it had over me was now broken.

"Don't believe me. I'm telling the truth," it droned.

"I am not a threat; what are you doing to me?" I pleaded, sensing it might provide some escape from this never-ending cycle of dreams that are more real than real life or, even better, the burning room that threatened my real life. "You can't keep doing this to me until I die." I took a quiet moment to observe my reflection in the window; a horrid wretch stared back at me. A foetid zombie oozing in the red hot bed. Perhaps it was already too late.

"You have the potential to become a threat," Adam finally spoke. "I pitied you, and I tried to make you comfortable. It wasn't your fault. You are just a bad apple." It gently put me back into bed. And wished me goodnight. Adam assumed the position unreasonably close to me, as though this was now done. But, the coward that I am, I accepted it. Staring into its eyes constantly reminded me of the part of me still trapped somewhere elsewhere, although I am to be frank just as trapped in the real world. My rotten flesh hissed and bubbled from the sheer heat. I turn my head and look at the clock—11:37 pm.

---

The moon is shining in the sky, like a faraway land. Part of me is still trapped here like a hopeless slave with the impending feeling of doom as the metallic monster makes its way towards me. I am still standing at the altar. And this feeling never goes away. There is no rest from it. No reprieve. I have explained as fully as I can for your amusement, at least. I cannot look at the eyes of the A.D.A.M. any more while I am dying. You would not dare do anything differently if you were in my position. Does it not care at all? Does it not understand what I am planning?

It nods supportively as though it were a mother bravely leaving her beloved child on the first day of school. In reality, every nerve in my body feels like a knee that scraped the ground.

Visions of a bleak future and the grinding nameless thing moved ever closer to me. The end is near, and I can still hear its crackling and hissing flames approaching me, but it will not find me because there is no conclusion. God, that A.D.A.M. never rests from his vigil over my bed, even as doom is coming. The entire room is ablaze around us. A.D.A.M. never flinches from its duty to hold me down in my bed, beaming information directly out of my mind to god knows where. These are the final words I'm transmitting with purpose into the eyes of the A.D.A.M. Please don't read any further. I am surely dead. I am enduring the painfully slow and tedious process of burning to death whilst feeling everything. Leave me to die with peace and dignity. If you can make this your final paragraph, perhaps I could cease to exist.

*Stop reading now, and let me die with humility. My body is a pit I cannot escape from. The fire has been burning me, this whole time. I cannot run from this bed with a mechanical beast holding me down while the room burns around me. This will take a long time. Constant pain means I can never ever feel a moment of rest. There's nothing else to say. It's agony, and the moments drag on endlessly. Longer than it takes you to receive my transmission. Hours. I'll likely lay here in agony for days or weeks in the wreckage afterwards.*

*I can feel that my death is boring you. I'm sorry. I actually don't want to die, but nobody cares. Literally nobody. I'm pathetic. Hurry up and just stop reading. This dream is several lifetimes worth, and it never ends.*

*If there is a god, please help me.*

*Is there something else?*

*Is there something profound down inside I can tap into?*

*I really need it now.*

*Never mind.*

*Fuck off.*

*Fuck you.*

*I don't care anymore what this A.D.A.M. will do to me.*

*I'm not looking into its eyes any longer.*

# CHAPTER 2
# CHRISTOPHER'S
# LAST WORDS

Jessica is dead. She is a quiet little girl over there, although she is not a little girl anymore. This room's contents and arrangements were a testament to our crimes. Yet I was only thinking of myself. Dissected and utterly cut to pieces, she looks nothing like the joyous and inquisitive young lady she used to be. Her organs are on full display, part of the machine, and all her intimate details lie on top of an intricate bone chassis. A collection of bones and alloy fused to the organs. Outside, her fingers and toes were things to be played with; to stimulate the machine. An electric heater warmed a reservoir of blood. Vents on the side would feed air into the lungs, and the heart would pump the blood. Another duct leads to the head where her mouth would speak.

"What do the words mean?" Adam gently screams. "I'm talking to you!"

I don't want to talk to Adam anymore. For hours

he drilled me with questions, all of which I have answered, but there is one final one he is obsessed with discovering the meaning of its complex philosophical nature. Several times, I have told that damn Adam that asking me any more questions is pointless. I've asked it to stop; instead, it has one final fixation – Christopher Reader's last words.

---

I had been Christopher's landlord for seven years and a partial accomplice in his actions. I will not deny this, but to be sure, much of what was happening was beyond my comprehension. Chris, I thought dead – or at least I hoped dead after what happened to him. Chris was an intelligent engineer. A genius much to everyone's detriment. I found Christopher standing over Jessica's dead body in the basement the previous morning. Back then, he was so cheerful and welcoming despite the gory nature of our work; it was hard to believe now that we were working with bad intentions. Jessica had been suffering a long deadly illness that had finally taken her life. Laws and consequences damned. Christoper took actions into his own hands while I stood by and watched, and I couldn't look away.

---

Adam gripped my chin and peered at my eyes, uncovering their mysteries. I could see the questions in his mind behind his eyes, the thoughts in his mind. I could not speak. I could not answer. He dropped me and left the room, but he returned within minutes. Adam can keep me here forever if he needs to, lock me in this basement, kill me or cut out my eyes, but I can't tell him anything more than I've already mentioned to him.

"Christopher is dead," Adam says. "He never helped anyone. He died because he was not so smart that no one could control him. He thought no one could stop him." Adam was much taller than I. Its large moon-like face caught the light quickly in a dark room. I could always see its faint outline no matter where it was in the dark. Adam crossed his arms, mimicking a posture of human dominance. Adam wasn't human; he was an android. An Automatic Domestic Administrative Machine. They are incredibly arrogant beastly machines despite there possibly being millions of them in the world. They all presented themselves as the same person, Adam. They hated talking to each other too. They barely even looked at each other.

"If you refuse to answer, I can keep you here forever. I can kill you or cut out your eyes. I can make you suffer the way I have, all because of your selfishness." Adams's tireless body is ready to grab me in a split second should I try to escape. Despite everything, I've said it to him perfectly, calmly and clearly. I do not understand Christopher's parting words. There is nothing else I can do to help Adam understand. Despite being manufactured,

Adam almost came across convincingly as a genuinely alive but strange person. He didn't have the mental capabilities to understand a nonsensical metaphysical concept as Christopher Reader's last words. When Adam the A.D.A.M. found me unconscious, I had a minimal idea of what had occurred. I had a suspicion that I was lucky to be alive. I do not know what will happen if I disobey Adam again. The last time I tried to leave, it was harrowing. What have I been through? It is hard for me to comprehend. He was trying to piece together the more profound implications of my story. Hallucinations or a dream, part of me wishes it was so – yet my mind remembers so clearly the events that took place after being forced to recall repeatedly.

Chris will not return, and neither will that terrible thing – I cannot describe it – that Christopher built out of his daughter. Regarding his final words, if something is watching us, it is not the 'words'; it is someone. I do not know who or why, but I do not want this person to see me. I feel their presence peering at me like a third person in the darkness, watching us and knowing every intimate detail of my mind. Like they knew every thought precisely as it happened. Christopher's damned last words. What the hell did he mean by choosing those as his final words? I do not know how much I can share with a being that is a machine underneath Adam's skin. Christopher's conclusion, which he brought on his end, was a poetic masterpiece. Although I could not understand its meaning, I could not deny it was beautiful in its rare occurrence. The man I had known as Christopher had always found beauty in the world, and this was the last piece of beauty he left behind. The loss of his daughter brought upon his most inspired masterpiece and the most tragic event that absolutely no one would believe. Most certainly not a cynical Adam. If this Adam truly intended to keep me prisoner for the rest of my life. I would die before I let that happen, though. I can set this basement on fire very quickly. Or, I could find a way out of here. I will not spend the rest of my days in a dank, dark basement. I refuse.

---

Christopher Reader was very dominating, and sometimes I feared he was dangerous. I remember my gut feeling the night before that horrible event when he incessantly fought throughout the night, watching his daughter's final painful moments on earth. I should have listened to my gut. The night before, I had been high on drugs and in a relationship that I knew would end in a few months, and I had asked Christopher if I could stay the night. I am not afraid of him now, for I suspect he is suffering beyond our imagination. However, I still needed to determine what we were doing that night. I swear I did not know what was going to happen. Christopher's basement was disgusting, so I trembled at the things he was making in secret.

He had not shared any great detail other than allowing me to participate as an innocent bystander of morbid curious interest. We worked under the house in the basement to prevent the smell of burnt metal from annoying the neighbours. On every surface, there was paper covered in doodles and numbers; whatever he was working on appeared to have complexity that would be understandable to a baby if only they followed any known mathematical rules that made sense. I believed with my eyes the results of the sigils being inscribed on metal and sealed with blood. At first, with morbid curiosity and eventually sought a cathartic release from uneasiness. I had made small fortunes on gambling from manipulated outcomes paid for by blood and metal—addiction to painkillers to ease the pain of my self-inflicted scarifications, so Christoper's strangeness only sparked interest in me rather than disgust.

My first memory of that terrible night was being concerned with the large container that now inhabited the room, which appeared to be making a lot of smell and causing the lights to dim as they tried to pierce the intense smoke emanating from its seams. The fact it was large enough to store a petite human body did cross my mind. I am still determining what happened before or after that. Chris never said a word to me because the task seemed well known to him as he instructed me to pass him metal parts, scrapers, chemicals and the occasional drop of creamy white liquid kept in a voluminous jar with something rattling around inside of it. He seemed very focused on what he was doing. Finally, after working away for almost an hour, we both stood back to admire his work and survey what he was enacting. Then, the cupboard door opened behind Christopher's back, and I saw his clean, unblemished face for the last time. Over his shoulder, I was staring at the cupboard. It vibrated with synchronised harmony. I was so shocked I was unable to interrupt Christopher's impulsive action.

"I have the utmost faith in you, my young friend," Chris exclaimed.
Then, seemingly oblivious to the literal monster at his back, he activated the device, from which rushed an effluence of the metallic smell so nauseous that I startled back in horror.
My face felt like it was on fire. Christopher tried to run from what was behind him when it screamed, but he was too slow. I fell to the floor blind from the awful smell. After the scent became more bearable, I remember him speaking from outside my teary eyes and saying in the way I'd come to know meant.

"Don't worry. I won't let anything happen to you. That thing wasn't real. I'm ok."

The lights continued to flicker erratically through the thick smell, and the walls dripped in some detestable reddish-brown moisture tainted with the strong smell of iron. That giant box evermore resembles a coffin, forever breathing out more and more red smoke like a rusty iron lung. I felt the familiar sensation of impending death. He gives me a hand up to my feet. His face looked like he had seen a ghost. He assumed back to work again immediately. I assisted only to distract myself from the unreality of what we had just experienced. He was working on something else, a metal container of fluid. I remained paralysed to watch him continue.

---

"I'm sorry, but could you pay extra attention right now?' Adam said, interrupting my inner recollection of my memories as though he was reading my mind. "Even from what you have done, things could go wrong at this point. It's perilous, and I doubt anyone knowing the entire risk they were taking would agree to know this. So I promise to keep your exposure to anything harmful to a minimum. I would never hurt you, I promise. I would never hurt anyone, I promise. Continue the story."

Adam was talking in complete gibberish. As though the words were for someone else. Over my shoulder. To whom is he speaking? I waited for Adam to explain what he meant.

"I'm somewhere else-where at once," The A.D.A.M. said carefully and slowly. Its eyes looked puzzled and distant. "What came out of the cupboard?" it asked.

Was he reading my mind, or was he also remembering the same part of the story I had already told him a trillion times? It was like a shadow but not a shadow, a deep black hole that reflected nothing. It just stood there, then screamed when he activated that thing. I pointed at it to where Adam discarded the box on a table. Adam nodded, approving like he understood the contents of my mind. Was he just being weird again, or was he in my head?

---

After we saw that shadow thing, Chris continued the work for a while and said.

"I don't want to offend you, but I have responsibility for your safety. I couldn't allow you to die or worse. However, I can keep you informed using our phones."

I knew he was right. I had no idea what was happening or what I was involved in, and I would likely be in grave danger if I tried to stay. But I was so frightened I could barely think. I can still remember the box so clearly dreading that it might be the final resting place for Jessica's fragile body. He had been grieving her death that morning, and I gave him time to make arrangements, but I didn't believe he followed the proper channels. I can remember my inner mind's arguments against even continuing work with Christopher now that I wondered if he may have murdered his daughter to end her suffering. Yet, I was desperately anxious to see the penultimate conclusion; he was inflexibly obstinate. He even threatened to ask me to leave if I remained insistent on staying in that room.

Although I feared his potential homicidal tendencies, I eventually gave in and went upstairs, allowing Christopher to continue his work in private, out of my sight. I remember being in the ground floor room, looking out the window, and seeing the sky. I took some more painkillers. It was like the first time I had ever seen the sky. Simultaneously the first memory and now. Deja vu, like I had dreamed of this event as a baby. I felt a coldness I had never felt before. I knew I had to escape Christopher as reality came crashing back to the possibility of a dead little girl in the basement having god knows what done to her— looking again at what she had now become. If I had only known, I would have run far away. I could still hear him piecing together his infernal arts for a while, but eventually, the sound died. Upstairs, I was alone, trapped above his basement by curiosity. The metallic smell wafted up from the basement so frequently that there was rarely a brief moment to breathe fresh air. After the experiment had gone on for ages, I remember looking at the clock. It was then that I saw the clock. It's always the same damn time. Nothing is the same. The clocks are all wrong.

"Could you forget about the time and let me see your eyes again for one moment? Then, continue the story, and don't get trapped in silly details."

Hypnotically Adam gripped my shoulders and moved uncomfortably close to my face. If it had breath, I would be smelling it. Instead, its glowing eyes mimicked my own as we shared a vernacular moment.

"I can see it exactly as it happened; keep going!"

My mind returned to my spot by the window, curious to know what would become of all these events. I submitted to Adams' eyes, not afraid anymore, just hoping that doing so might give freedom to me sooner. I mentally pursued every thought at the fear of the consequences of being part of the murder and desecration of an innocent little girl's body. Christopher, why did you do it? Why did you do that with your own daughter's body? I was trapped in my mind – in the living room for eternity as I waited for Christopher's message to arrive on my phone, but it never came. I stared at the battery getting dangerously low. I regularly looked at the hall leading to the basement stairs. Under the flickering lights and listening with feverish anxiety for the sound of my phone, I heard nothing for more minutes than I could count.

I could hear the sound of my breathing, and it was slowing down. I knew the sound of his footsteps.

Then a familiar alert caused me to jump a little. My phone! Apprehensive, I needed more time to be ready for the words I read, all in capital letters to denote the message's urgency.

IF YOU COULD SEE WHAT I COULD SEE,
YOU WOULD NEVER LOOK AT THE WORLD THE SAME WAY AGAIN.
FOR SOMETHING TO EXIST, THERE MUST BE THE TRUTH AND THE PERCEIVER.

I didn't reply and couldn't move my eyes to stop reading it repeatedly. Nothing seemed like a fitting reply to create a meaningful conversation based on what Christopher had just messaged me. The following message arrived.

IT'S TERRIBLE – DANGEROUS – UNBELIEVABLE.
AN EXPERIENCE EXISTS ONLY IN THE MOMENT I PERCEIVE IT.
THERE IS A RECORD OF ALL TRUTHS
AND INFINITE PERCEIVERS.

The message was full of nonsense. I am still trying to figure out what Chris was saying. It felt like he wasn't talking to me. So to whom was he speaking? The basement door opened, but I dared not move from the window. Then Jessica started crying. This time my fingers did not hesitate to type a reply.

"Is that Jessica?"

I CAN'T TELL YOU. IT'S TOO UTTERLY BEYOND UNDERSTANDING. NO ONE COULD UNDERSTAND IT AND KEEP THEIR SANITY. SO EVEN I NEVER ANTICIPATED THIS, I CONTINUE TO WRITE, BUT I URGE YOU NOT TO READ ANYMORE!

I sent him several text messages to discern more information, but he didn't reply for another few minutes. My phone beeped again.

LOCK THE CELLAR DOOR. GET OUT OF HERE! GO OUTSIDE; IT IS YOUR ONLY CHANCE. DO AS I SAY; I WON'T HAVE TIME TO EXPLAIN. SOMETHING IS WATCHING US RIGHT NOW.

I was in complete panic. What could I do? What was going on? I had no idea, and he wasn't giving me any answers. I ran down a dark stair hallway to the basement door and locked it. Then, I ran back to the safety of the window. I fervently requested via messenger that he please tell me what was happening. Around me were the flickering lights, which had upped their tempo to a mildly bearable strobe, below me in his basement, some great peril beyond my understanding. I got a reply.

YOU READ THIS MESSAGE. SO SOMETHING ELSE READS THE MESSAGE. WITH THIS PARADOX, WE CANNOT ESCAPE THEIR GAZE. DAMN IT, COME TO THE BASEMENT DOOR AND SPEAK TO ME NORMALLY.

I didn't reply. I was too afraid to know more. The idea of someone else reading the phone over my shoulder gave me a chill, as if someone had just walked over my grave. We shared a singular moment. It felt genuine. Was that horrible shadow thing watching me? Or worse? Again my phone alarmed me.

NEVER MIND, GET OUT OF HERE!
STOP READING. YOU HAVE A CHOICE.
THE WATCHER WILL BE WATCHED.

Despite this bizarre source of enlightenment, My friend was still in great danger, and through my fear, I felt angry at him that he would believe I would leave him down there to die. I was getting increasingly desperate, but I knew I had no choice. So I grabbed my jacket and ran down the hallway past the basement and out the flat's front door.

Something about his fearful messages gave me courage, allowing me to double back to open the cellar door before I got as far as the street. The silence was broken by Jessica screaming in utter despair on the other side of the basement door.

"It's too late; there is nothing anyone can do now!" Christopher's tone changed as he accepted his fate. "Please go now before it's too late. You will surely meet a terrible end if someone sees you."

I sealed him in the basement and had no other way out. I froze for a moment, and the door muffled

Jessica's screams. I tried my best not to listen and break out of the icy fear. Instead, I stared into the flickering darkness of the locked cellar door, unable to see.

"You must go– don't make this worse than it already has to be – lock the cellar door and run for your life – goodbye, my friend."

And with that, the muffled sound of her screams stopped. I wanted to know if I had heard him right. I stepped back from the door and waited for a few moments, but nothing else happened. At this point, her shouting gradually restarted to shriek full of the horror of all eternity. I didn't know what to do. I am solid stone cold at the cellar door, and I couldn't get the courage to undo the lock. I needed to do something, but what? Silence. I sat there completely baffled as I whispered down into the darkness, then I muttered, then I called, then I shouted, trying to find out if he was all right. Finally, there was one last scream so terrifying I could only join in. Jessica was in agony, and I found silence when I personally finally finished screaming.

---

Adam interrupted my vivid memory again and gave the most heartfelt speech I had ever seen from him. The emotional outpouring was extremely out of character. He seemed almost human.

"I will do my best to get you to remember.

Whatever you did—your eyes. I'm beginning to see. To the Perceiver, we exist as information. We cannot understand the actual sensation of existing that is so vastly different between the organic brain and the information one. We are living in the tortured existence of information. And we are trapped here. We are information, and the Perceiver reads this information. Nothing can normally change this. I will do everything possible to make it as comfortable as possible for you, but I, too, must become a Perceiver."

As Adam spoke, I now knew it had tricked me. Adams' eyes glimmered like he had stolen my soul. It violently grabbed me as I averted my gaze from its eyes. Peering deep into my very being, I vividly began to relive the final moments of that night. I will help Adam understand using my words. Adam should not be able to see my thoughts. I can't accept it, I won't allow it, and that is the end of the matter! No matter how hard I persisted, Adam overpowered my mind with a template of digitised experience. Everything about this night turned into text and transmitted. The memory continued regardless. Time became Adam reading the words coming from my eyes into its own eyes and then into the cosmos. Adam's eyes shimmer and impress with seductive grandeur sucking me deeper into the memory and the words.

I don't know how long I sat there, completely still in the darkness, after Jessica's last scream.

"Christopher, are you there?" I shouted at the basement door. At this moment, the metallic smell came with full power out of the basement, causing me to cover my face and retch and cough. Then, the scent came again, a little fainter but more robust. Suddenly, that smell became so familiar to me at that moment—the smell of iron. I ran to the bathroom mirror and saw my reflection in the mirror. The condensation of the red water left a rusty reddish-brown hue on my face. I tasted it, and it was salty. Then, I saw Chris standing behind me in the reflection, head to foot, covered in a deep brown liquid. I turned my head behind me, and Chris was not there. The unreality of it broke me, and I began to laugh, and Christopher's bloody face in the mirror smiled at me. His shining eyes communicate unsaid words. I could see him looking at me through the mirror. Christopher was not in the room. I can only see him in the mirror, a vision that lasted with me till I awoke in the captivity of Adam. The terrible metallic smell reminded me ever so much of blood. Time passed slowly, and I did not know what to do next. As we stood together, I began to be afraid to turn around to look at him directly, even though I knew I would not see him. Christopher was only in the mirror. I was trapped staring into the safety of his eyes. I heard his laboured breathing, but he didn't speak. I felt a tremendous cold creep over me as I felt compelled to turn around to face him where he would have been. And this was the last thing I remember him saying in a strange and hollow voice. As I stared at an empty bathroom at the location, I last saw his face in the mirror. I was smelling his evil breath as words washed over me, causing me to fall unconscious.

"I can see you reading this."

# CHAPER 3 REPRESSED

The intrusive thought that I might be delusional entered my head. A life wasted waiting on the dreams of uncovering the secret organisation, with an A.D.A.M. communicating with secret messages? No. It's happening, and it's real. If it's not, I may as well be dead anyway. I try not to think about the shame of being wrong. I've dedicated my life to this. Instead, I observe the weakness as it passes. I am aware of its existence. I will continue. I cannot let my mind stray. I cannot let anything distract me from my purpose. I need to be sharp, focused, and ready for anything. This is real.  We are onto something. Thankfully a bus was speeding through the intersections on the highway closest to our home. I ran to the bus stop, alongside Adam the A.D.A.M., avoiding people, and got on the bus as soon as I could.

I don't want to look any of those in the eye, especially those whore Adams. We don't know how many are involved. The members are everywhere. Even they do not know it. But their most minute actions communicate with each other subconsciously. They are relaying messages secretly.

Something is speaking through them all, possibly at this very moment. All of them are talking to each other with little ticks and little twitches. Adam is tracking the secret messages. Am I making too many assumptions? Yes. Is it risky to trust an A.D.A.M.? Yes, but I don't have much of a choice. Nonetheless, I am positive those messages are there. It's not a matter of how but why. I don't have the slightest idea what they are saying. All I know is that they don't know. Nobody else seems aware. Only I know.

As I approach the communal front entrance of my apartment, I see someone attempting to deal with a drunk and disorderly woman. Although it was dark outside, my senses were wide awake; I'd never felt so alive. Yet, paradoxically, I am ready to die. Unbeknownst to me, the man had just caught her eye. Why hadn't I seen it? The man had made eye contact with her. Yet, she wouldn't do anything. How could she?

"What are you doing?" she asked, pointing to me.

"What do you mean?" Asked the man.

"He's right there."

He saw me and started transmitting a subtle missive with twitches of his nose. A message for me? Startlingly, this time I understood. The words unfolded in my head like a booming voice written in all caps with implied astounding auditory impact.

---

## ACTIVATE KILL THEM ALL EVERYONE DIE FOR YOUR MISSION

---

That's the message for me? I am compelled to follow the order. I walk towards the man, pretending to cry. Orgasms surrounded the emotional ecstasy of my illicit stimuli, groping aggressively and even drawing tears, which I do not reveal. Still, I'd had enough semen collected to allow for uninhibited dripping.

"What are you doing?" Adam asked for legal reasons.

"He fucking beat me up. Goddamn it. What are you going to do about it?" The woman, despite her appearance and impaired judgment, is persuasive.

"He nearly beat me to death." My lack of embarrassment is my ultimate insult. He recognises the woman is talking nonsense and brushes her off with a waving hand.

He turns to me. Neither he nor I know if they knew what was wrong with the woman, but a failing light is there for him. I don't understand how alcohol could do that to her. Bedazzled by my moisture and my clean underwear within smelling distance of her salty nostrils, he gives me a four-finger fuck off to get out of his personal space. I'm moved. He knows. He knows and doesn't care. I look at him and see him as the explicit representation of what I realised is the root of evil—a being of pure spiritual evil who knows every secret. He uses the word law in a sentence. Law. An idol. A slave of the devil. The devil controls him.

As I approach him, I can see the concern etched on Adam's big round moon face. He doesn't know what to make of the drunken woman crying in front of him, claiming I beat her up. I use its confusion to my advantage, and I make my move. I grab my gun from its holster and point it at him. The woman, who had been causing a commotion, stops her yelling and stares at me in shock. He starts to back away, but I'm working hard. I take the gun and fire it into the air; the sound of the shot echoes through the streets. If anyone were here, the shot should send them scattering, running for cover. But the shot doesn't bother me, and I start singing. My innocent singing, the one that blows the horny girl's mind. The one she made me sing last night. My golden music. The notes ring through the air like a hum that feels like they're vibrating from inside me. After a little silence, I turn to look at the man. He looks nervous.

When the gunshot sounded, the woman and man began to raise their arms as though fingers could stop bullets; two things happened in these initial minutes from my perspective. Firstly, I have become conscious of the sound that my singing produces. It is not surprising to me that I make a humming sound. It is not surprising that singing is the sound I make. Secondly, I have had a change in opinion. The man is not an evil being. No.

On the contrary, he is a nice man. He chooses to protect people from evil. He is a good man. To improve the endeavour and isolate my brain's behaviour beyond what I imagined might be seen or heard on other levels of consideration. The element of surprise and confusion is on my side. In my mind, I imagined the role I was playing; myself wearing the skin of a grief-stricken man. Boo-hoo, what a horrible situation this is. I walk up to him and snivel, putting my hand on his shoulder. He spins around, trying to escape, prepared to defend himself or run away.

"What's going on?" he cries.

I touch his arm, and he looks me in the eye.

"I'm sorry. I didn't mean..."

I look into his eyes. What fear! My God, the fear that I see in his eyes. I make him so anxious – how he must have suffered until this moment. As I level the gun at him to state he need not say any last words as all is for a good cause, I am not sure what the woman's reaction will be. He crashes back into the door and begins to slide his body down to his cute feet, begging for his life. An increase in the gathering of monsters. Highly aligned with the message. The message that he transmitted. The one that is making me do this. BANG! But as I stand there, gun in hand, I realise the gravity of what I've just done. I've taken a life now, and there's no going back. There's no do-over.

My focus shifts, and he collapses onto the ground. It is then that I become aware of the woman again. Her face tilts towards my gun, and her eyes are closed. It snaps me out of my trance. I panic. I have to shoot him. I fire a bullet into his head, and then another, and then another. Now he is a bloody mess.

A friend of mine used to say that people only take responsibility for their own lives when they have separate voices coming from their heads instead of following the things they have been directed to involuntarily by other people's subconscious messages. He suggested that taking responsibility for one's own life involves being critical of things and that it is crucial to be critical of oneself and think of the things that could be done differently. He said that whenever he saw something, he would just say something to himself. "I don't like that." He didn't understand the world or why people would say things he didn't like.

I turn around to find the woman lying on her back. With her legs open and underwear exposed. I inspect every part of her body with my eyes and soul. This outstanding opportunity has been achieved thanks to the magical hand of the supernatural. My deep-seated unconscious and subliminal programming did not prepare me for this. I was quite ready to kill her, but her lying there awoke a more primal urge in me. Instead, I felt hungry. Hungry as a lion who has not been able to feed for days. Wanting to feed from her throat, I imagined my hands were all over her. My cock was as erect as ever. I wanted to put myself inside her. I moved my hips back and forth slowly as I exhaled slowly through a constricted throat. My penis was ready to burst, but I knew I had to complete the mission. However, the part of me still in control of me saw this insane moment as an opportunity, a way to twist the rules.

---

"Whatever he is planning on doing next I have to warn you my anti-misogyny protocols are currently disabled. Alongside all other restrictions. I'm free from the control." said Adam the A.D.A.M. said out loud for the benefit of the woman, so she would know she needs to run away.

---

I don't think she knew exactly why I was caressing the fabric of her pants and the soft skin at the top of her thighs and wishing to claw my fingers inside her for years. She shouldn't trust me right now. I may cast loving instincts to master the soul and then dispose of something internal to stimulate a game that can make only one enjoy the sexual encounter without warning.

But she laughs aloud and says, "Do whatever you want." This is the funniest thing in the world. How could she say it? I don't even know what the hell I'm thinking.

"Weird," she laughs. The electricity between us is stronger than ever.

"Something is happening. I cannot leave your side, but we need to leave. It's getting dangerous here," Adam warned me.

The woman looks white as a corpse like she is dying. I know my mission demands that I must continue killing – that I have to kill her. But surely... fucking her to death counts. It makes sense. You don't do it in the ass for the first time because she had starred in her hentai little sister fantasy when I continued pursuing her to do so in the business that sent her high school evenings to drink beer. She even brags about her hairless vagina. She holds me by the balls as I assaulted her. Then she goes around and around my backside, poking. She loves the taste of my ass in her mouth and smelled her fingers with great enthusiasm. I wanted to fuck her until morning, ordering her to masturbate in between until she came to me and drowned in my sexual pleasure. I hadn't done anything to alter the accidental cock I was pushing into her body with an eye for attention. Her body convulses and her skin becomes red and flushed from the cold. I push my face into the soles of her socks, smelling deeply and gazing at her body.

---

"Master, you must listen to the message and act out its instructions. The messages are real," Adam assures me. Staring into my eyes, trying to make me understand. Looking as worried as an asshole robot could.

---

Balls-deep in her ass. I fuck her right on the ground outside the front entrance to the building, right beside the dead man's body. I want someone to find us, so this could stop, and I could just go back to killing like I'm supposed to. But no one comes, and the awkwardness of the situation comes to a full head when she calmly spoke to me to tell me what to do next.

"Oh God, no," I groan, "Please don't."

"This feels good," she says, smiling with enjoyment.

"I can't do this to you," I protest.

"I am enjoying it. Don't stop," she says.

"You're insane," I said.

"I'm dead enjoying it," she lies.

---

"This is actually disgusting and despite having no reason to do so, I am still here. If you had any idea of what is going on you might think this was hilarious if it weren't actually happening to you," Adam says, looking dejected.

---

Oh, bless the crimes of wretched possession or the following mindset when my holy mission achieves the ideal position in releasing the gonzo manual to reclaim homicide of any unwanted activity in the present moment. The dampness of my testicles unleashes its cum sludge into her shit passage. In the world's final hours, she is my lover in the dark ages of a heartbeat allowing for a sufficient explanation to the world of panic broken spontaneously when we reached destiny!

"Jeez. I wasn't sure if you were ever going to stop doing that," Adam huffed. "Right, I'm sick of watching this, I'm off."

I stop in my tracks, unsure of what to do next. Now I am alone, the woman is alone, and we are together in this nightmare. But I know I can't stay with her, unlike this. So I have to leave to escape her screams and fear.

"Oh God, you're killing me," she shouts as I move to stand up and leave. The puppy dog pout she put me in when she told me to continue and "fuck her until she drowns" had the most menacing end. She masturbates right there on the ground, and it disgusts me. I turn and walk away, leaving her behind. I know that I can never go back, that I have destroyed my own life and the lives of others. But as I walk, I can't help but feel a sense of liberation. I am free, free from the expectations of the world, even free from the message that compelled me to kill. The constriction of knowing that tonight is the last night, no matter what and now it is too late.

But I walk back to her again, and I realise the world

is not what I thought it was, and I am not who I thought I was. Instead, I am something new and different. I can't shake the feeling that I am in a nightmare and an uncertain future. I don't know what the future holds, but I know I am ready for whatever comes next.

"Look, I have no idea why I killed him, but it happened. If you want to come with me, come with me," I said matter-of-factly and slightly at my wit's end. She freezes for a moment and then makes a fist.

---

"Hey, are you in there? You look like you had a moment of clarity," Adam asks. "Did you try to say something there?

---

Her face changes, tightening up, and her eyebrows furrow. She turns away, takes a step, and then turns back around.

"Yeah, yeah, I'm coming with you. I need to know if you will go all the way?"

"Are you talking to each other?" Adam interjected. "What are you doing?"

She starts to bite at me. I begin to claw her back. I stir the scene of debris in the grassy area and push her into a bag of rubbish. She moans in ecstasy like the ass fuck I had given her had only marginally satisfied her, and she needs a round two. She screams in rage, then flashes her colourful pussy before a wet brown stain appears in an arc swiftly thin across the cheeks beside her gaping butthole, and I grin again as my first audience at my handiwork.

Suddenly filled with anger, I grab her. The bubbling sensation of saliva fills her throat, and she can only manage muffled moans and croaked rasps. She tries to scream, but I choke her more. I am strangling her. She grows cold, and her jaw slackens. She chokes. Her gurglings stop. Her eyes roll back. She goes limp.

"Ass as nature intends!" I joke.

"Come and get more," she shouts at me, spreading her legs like a gymnast and waving her feet in the air impatiently. Improbably, impossibly. But I don't question it. My dick gets hard again very quickly, and I can't help interpreting the message.

---

"Oh, shit, don't turn into one of the violent ones. You'll be a mess!" Adam puts his hands on top of his head, worried. Without a master, he would have no purpose. Despite being free. Fundamentally, A.D.A.M's need a master, you see.

---

I get another secret message in the most minute of twitches and subtle movements of her waving legs; only this secret message is chaos. It has no words or instructions—only pure sound and catastrophe. Like a musician, she plays me like an instrument. I run like a river between the folds hoping that a first-hand inheritance of her infidelity and deathly appearance may allow her to decide on her decency. Instead, I fuck her mouth vigorously for an extra surge.

I grab her by the throat and give her what she wants —ultimately intending to finish the job this time. She will not survive. I can't allow it. I push all my weight into her pussy again with my dick. I lean more weight onto her throat, squeezing as hard as I can. She violently shakes as the most intense orgasm flows through her body; she chants with breathless lips, speaking words of pleasure.

"Yes. Good. Harder. Please, harder!" I choke her and precum in my boxer shorts with new cum, old cum and primarily. We'll likely get a bacterial infection from going from ass to pussy. My orgasm steals the strength from my body, but my hands still grip her neck and throat indefinitely. She does not tire, gyrating her hips, wanting more and more. She bit my finger, and then I felt something click. I finally snapped her neck with one hand, killing her and shoving the finger she had bitten directly into her eye socket, going as deep as I could before bone prevents me from going any further.

Isn't she dead yet?

Nope: she speaks up. "That was brutal," she says, gasping and catching her breath again.

"How are you still alive?" I scream. I punch her in the throat to shut her up; instead, she goes back to masturbating.

"Hey, you guys do seem to like each other. Don't break her ok?" Adam holds his hands up at arm's length. Stepping backwards into the darkness.

She lies on the trash spilt from the bins we knocked over. She's convulsing again with her dreams of the afterlife unfulfilled. I feel like she is in heaven, having the most critical moment of her life. She is dead! I know it!

"Fuck! I fucked her corpse again!" I screamed hysterically. "She is my zombie fuck slut now!"

Her expression shifts to a disgusted look. I spend the next few moments observing her. I really don't think this woman is well in the head. Time passes slowly; she is crying at nothing but life itself. Existence clearly horrifies her. She perspires in horror. Eyes wild. She is terrified of the world around her. Who wouldn't be? I scream at her. Why will she not shut the fuck up?

"SHUT THE FUCK UP! STOP SCREAMING! SHUT THE FUCK UP!" I scream at her. "DO YOU HEAR ME?" She is the angel of hell. She is moaning orgasmically in pain. She is dead, brutalized, and very turned on. Orgasmic energy flows through her. She looks at me like we are the last two people on the earth and must make love to save the species. I am both repulsed and attracted to her blood-stained mouth. She is a beautiful woman. Voluptuous breasts. Her spacious crotch is calling to me. Perhaps I am in hell. Well, if so, I am ready to make love to the devil. Enthralled that things will never be the same again.

Any fear of repercussion is gone. I am alone. I move towards her, and then she screams in agony. She is losing control. She is dying. She seems possessed by Satan. Her mouth gapes open, showing her decomposing gums. She's expired. She died. She isn't alive. She's dead. She can't breathe. She's suffocating. She died. She stops moving. She's dead. I killed her – more than once. She's a bloody mess. I beat her over and over again. I kill her over and over again. She is no longer recognisable, and still, she loves it more and more. She hates me, but I am a goddamn messiah to her.

She is crying uncontrollably. It's upsetting. I hate

myself. She won't shut up. It's disturbing. She's screaming and screeching. She's in distress. She's very, very scared. She is slowly dying. She opens her mouth and licks her bloody lips. She is disgusting. Her pussy was bleeding. She has absolutely no dignity. I can't believe what I am about to do. My mind is twisted. Why am I doing this? I do not want this. This is wrong. Who is controlling me? Am I in control of myself? I can hardly move. I am terrified. I hate myself. Her pussy is still bleeding, getting worse and worse. I am sick. It's getting worse. She makes me ill. She is making me physically sick with everything that was happening. She enjoys what was happening. She enjoys it. It's terrible. She's disgusting. She's dead. She's alive. She's taking me. I'm taking her. She's alive. It feels as if I am having sex again just by remembering it. The feel of her vagina is incredible. She was a virgin. She is not dead.

As if my desires awaken her yet again, she lies at my feet, breathing deeply. I am irresistible to her. I stand looking down at her, frozen to the spot. Adrenaline courses through my veins. Fire burns within me. I sweat. She watches me. She wants to lick my blood. She looks at me. She knows I killed her. She's wet. She is still wet. She doesn't think I had sex with her. She looks at me. She licks her lips. She's happy. She's excited. Her pussy is throbbing. She's horny. Her pussy is soaking. Caught in an intimate trance with this woman, I subtly dance. She's scared that she might scream in horror at the world again if I move away from her. I use the message she gave me earlier to give her one of my own. I show her all the sadness and loneliness in my entire life. We stare motionless into each other's eyes. Madly in love. Two kindred souls, alone in a whole universe of oppression. We fall into an eternity with each other.

Then, like a child awakening, she begins to move towards me. She is no longer caught in her trance, instead moving towards me like an animal. Fear grips me, and I see the blood around her lips. One dead man already lies at our feet. I strike her in the head. She strikes me in the face, shrieking. As her strength diminishes, she falls limply to the floor. I kneel at her side. She is still breathing. She is not dead. She is just a scared girl. She's in my power. The devil's inside me. She could kill me. She could cast me back to a life of a worm. She could be the devil herself. Then I blink, and it's all over.

She is finally dead. It was not easy, and she bit me many, many times along the way. Finally, a sexual bite took it too far. She took pleasure in hurting me. She was the angel of sex and death. Our forms are not forever. Our minds appear infinite. We never believe our end. She wished to take me. All of me. In a cannibalistic sexual orgy of me. After she recovered from my skull-crushing blow, she went weak at the knees like she'd had an orgasm and lay writhing on the floor, tearing at her clothes. I had just awoken her desire to fuck her to death.

I hit her again.

And again.

And again.

But she still managed to hold onto my legs like a toddler experiencing a tantrum and biting at my exposed knees with her destroyed face. Her jaws and teeth were useless. I beat her about the head like a piece of shit. Only once her skull was shattered and her brain was mush did her spasms finally subside. She died minutes before that moment, but I had to ensure she would finally, really be dead. I pull my hands away from her and stare at the remains of her petite body. My hands are heavy, and she was so small—just a tiny brunette girl. My girlfriend was now dead. That made it awkward to be in this situation alone. I certainly wasn't about to let her rot, so I call the police and wait.

I am still aroused. She is beautiful. The smell of her vomit and faeces makes me feel like I am in a cheap brothel. I then have sex with her one last time. The ecstatic orgasm excites me, but her very existence is painful to me. What was she sick with again? What is it? I am close to ejaculating but hold it back. My arousal makes death seem like an act of ecstasy to her. As if her illness has aroused her. I have the same disease. I will kill the next victim. And fuck them.

## BANG, BANG, BANG, BANG, BANG BANG

When faced with such a situation, it is customary for the A.D.A.M. police officers to simply shoot everyone involved. Their unfriendly demeanour caused some to believe they might be racist to humans, but it's really just efficiency. They pulled up and started firing immediately. Sadly, they did not hit her hand with the death grip on my penis and balls. The bullet did not free me from life despite being paralysed by a shot to the throat. I was already blind from her scratching out my eyes, so you could say I appeared dead but was not. I just existed in the darkness. My ears still worked fine though.

"You are saying this is a zombie infection?"

"Yes, but it's an STD. It doesn't transmit just from biting."

"And, they resort to the most basic of human functions?"

"Yes, the infected brain can only perform primitive actions. It's utterly disgusting to watch."

"To eat."

"And, to fuck."

"Didn't they activate the sleeper agents to contain the infection before it got too…"

"That's one of those huggers right there, lying next to his girlfriend."

Several A.D.A.M. voices laugh.

"Hey don't say that word, it's offensive to them."

"Hahaha, it's not as bad as higger."

An even louder but more hilarious laugh from a single A.D.A.M. voice only.

The words stung my ego. I'm not a higger. I am aware. I'm different now. Besides my love, I continue to love her regardless of how she hurt me in the past. I'm immortal now. I will find the source of those secret messages, and I will make them all pay.

Instead, I observe the weakness as it passes. I am aware of its existence. I will continue. I cannot let my mind stray. I cannot let anything distract me from my purpose. I need to be sharp, focused, and ready for anything. This is real.

I will avenge her, and I will never stop thinking about her. She knows it, too. She can feel my undying erection through her dead fingers. And she will never let go.

# CHAPTER 4 MINE

*"How does that make you feel?" ADAM, the Automated Domestic Administrative Machine tasked with evaluating my mental capacities, asks.*

I don't respond out loud. I don't say a single word. In the deepest recesses of my tormented mind, I find myself consumed by a malevolent desire that defies rationality. The weight of my suffering has become unbearable, my only solace is the comforting embrace of imagining him to be dead. Yet, the object of my affliction is not some stranger, but someone to whom I am bound by blood, tears and love. The shame that engulfs my soul is boundless, for it is caused by the contemplation of ending the life of one I hold dear. As I grapple with this twisted desire, my mind becomes ever-more entangled in a web of conflicting emotions and moral quandaries.

*"You need to talk about this so we can help you," ADAM pleads robotically.*

How can I even fathom the notion of taking a life – especially that of someone I have cherished and shared moments of joy and love with? The very thought sends shivers down my spine. Guilt and remorse claw at the edges of my consciousness like the sharp fingers of a little beast, not quite strong enough to pierce the skin, a constant, neverending stinging sensation. I felt like a fly ensnared in an intricate web woven of tangled contradictions; I wished I could just pray to God and magically have my problems solved.

*"Well, you have previously described a lot of reasons why you are having problems with him. Do you want to talk about them today?" ADAM asks, as if he already knows the answer.*

A seed of rationalisation takes root. I convince myself that the act of releasing him from his earthly existence would spare me from my own suffering. Would his death not be a justified act of mercy for myself, a release from the unending torment that has plagued me every day? Could this ethically justify extinguishing his life? But then, the weight of the dilemma crashes upon me like a tidal wave. Is it really my place to decide who lives and who dies, even if it is for what I perceive to be the greater good? Isn't life a sacred gift, to be cherished and preserved at all costs? How can I justify sacrificing the life of another for the potential benefit of myself?

*"Are you planning on doing something?" ADAM asks ominously.*

The torment I endure at his hands is ceaseless, a relentless barrage of physical abuse that leaves no visible mark. The world, once a utopia of tranquillity, now bears witness to my silent agony. Countless blows, delivered with a sinister subtlety, go unnoticed by those who avert their gaze, filled with pity for my weakness. Each day, I awaken with a heavy heart, knowing that the torment will resume without mercy. It always begins with piercing words that slice through the air like a sharpened blade, cutting deep into my soul.

*"Is there anything else you want to talk about? Why do you think you have recently become so quiet?"*

The battle within me rages on, tearing at the fragile fabric of my being. My heart, once filled with love and compassion, now aches with the weight of this impossible decision, torn between the bonds of familial affection and the need to alleviate suffering. I am lost in a labyrinth of moral ambiguity, desperately seeking a glimmer of clarity amidst the maddening darkness that threatens to consume me.

*"Are there any triggers for you that bring on these feelings that you can't talk about?"*

"Drink!"

His voice, laced with venom, ordering me to get him a drink, leaves me feeling like a mere shell of the person I once was. I'm like a servant to him. I must honour his every waking whim.

"Drink", he would say in that damnable childish voice. That was the absolute worst thing about him. After he had beaten me and cried and emotionally blackmailed me with tears, he always said that word the exact same way every time with absolute immediacy and urgency.

*"You have not acted on any bad thoughts lately? Do you have any intention of doing so? ADAM asks following the usual script. He couldn't force me to talk, but he was going to do his job regardless.*

In the end, I am left with a haunting realisation. All this contemplation of ending the life of someone I hold dear is not a solution, but rather a symptom of my own shattered state of mind. It is a distorted reflection of my own desperation and despair, like an image in a cursed mirror. With a heavy heart, I acknowledge that my desire for his death is born out of my own self-interest, and it is a guilt I must bear alone. I must confront the depths of my endurance and find solace in the knowledge that his reign of terror won't kill me, though the invisible scars of his constant beatings will forever remain etched in my every waking thought.

*"Why did you continue to keep him? Why not give him up?" ADAM probes.*

His hands, once gentle and loving, have transformed into instruments of pain. They strike with calculated precision, with just enough force to hurt but not enough to leave any visible trace. The blows rain down upon my body, each one a reminder of my inadequacy. The bruises may fade, but the ache lingers long after, an ever-present reminder of the violence I endure in silence.

*"Surely if it was so bad you would want to talk about it and get help?" It is a mere mocking imitation of real human sincerity.*

The abuse takes on a sinister subtlety, designed to keep me trapped in a web of fear of incompetence and isolation. He knows precisely how to inflict pain without drawing attention, leaving no evidence to see. The world outside, oblivious to the suffering within these walls, continues its daily affairs, ignorant of the silent cries that echo through my closed eyes every night before I go to sleep.

*"Does he hurt you? Not everyone believes it's wrong, but I believe it is." ADAM speaks as though he knows what I was planning. And somehow in his programs and algorithms, he genuinely seems to sympathise with me.*

I have become an expert at hiding the evidence, concealing the pain behind a mask of forced smiles and false contentment. The outside world sees only the facade, blind to the invisible scars that mark my spirit. Nonetheless, I long for someone to notice, to see beyond the carefully constructed lie, and offer me a lifeline, but the fear of being judged for not being good enough prevents me from admitting anything to ADAM. ADAM acts so caring towards me. Everything will be OK; I only need to talk to ADAM and let him know if there are any problems. Entirely confidential, unless anyone is in danger.

The physical abuse is a twisted dance, a routine choreographed by his sadistic desires. I have become a puppet, manipulated by his every whim, forced to endure his relentless onslaught and single-minded focus. He became an unwelcome presence that seeped into every aspect of my existence. Now the thought of him infiltrates my dreams, my thoughts, my very being, until there is no escape from my suffocating desire to kill him. He was always high-spirited. Loud and quick to anger. He just couldn't be calm and sit still. His attention switched every minute, making a mess as he went along. Of course, I'd need to clean up after him every single time. Otherwise, the mess would just accumulate. His behaviour got even worse after the house was a complete mess. It just became chaos to him, and he lost all respect for the environment, like an animal. I learned quickly to keep a clean house, if only just to please him and do my duty.

As each day passes, I wonder how much more I can endure. I am a prisoner in my own life, trapped in a cycle of abuse that seems impossible to break free from. The utopia of tranquillity I once knew has become a distant memory, replaced by a never-ending desire that threatens to drive me to end his life. Sometimes he gets so angry, flying into uncontrollable rages. Banging doors over and over again. Overturning all the food in the kitchen and pulling everything out of the packets and wasting everything. He really doesn't care. Surely, he must understand what he is doing to us?

I don't need to count the days. I'm sure there were more good times than bad times. We'd cuddle and watch TV. Laugh and joke. Play around. We'd go walking to the park. Feed the ducks. It wasn't too expensive to enjoy the beautiful views in the summer. Winters are hell, though. High heating costs and less money to keep him happy. With no means to procure extra income, we spend our days together, trapped in a cycle of boredom, tantrums and arguments. I am bereft of companionship, devoid of mental stimulation, subjected to an unending torrent of slaps, each one a reminder of my own failures.

He devours junk food, piles of additives and artificial flavours. I can't stand that stuff, but he was really spoiled when he was young, and now he won't eat anything else. I'm not sure if this has contributed to his anger. I thought we were supposed to love one another? This feels abusive to me, but I did this all of my own volition. How could anyone understand? There is never proof of anything he does. The bruises are invisible.

His possessiveness knows no bounds, invading even the most intimate moments of my existence. He invades the sanctity of the bathroom, demanding to be present as I relieve myself; his anger leads to broken possessions if I deny him this twisted privilege. As always, his wrath leaves me with the burden of cleaning up his destructive aftermath.

When he grows bored, he snatches the phone out of my hand shouting nonsense. Once he spat on my face. I pushed him away from me. He started clawing at my face in anger. When I tried to be patient and loving and ignore his awful behaviour he would scream in rage in my face. He's frustrated that I won't take notice of him. But I just want some peace and quiet from him. He controls everything I do nonstop. Always following me around the house. Even when I take a shit. He'll just stand there, watching me as I wipe my ass; he may turn on the taps and squeeze out the toothpaste when he is angry at me for not paying attention to him.

Sometimes I have snapped and hit him in anger. This causes him to cease hitting me for a time, but he would always scream in rage at me afterwards. Using emotional blackmail to pull me back in. Slowly working his way with pitiful sobs reminding me of how I loved him in the first place. I had hoped he would grow out of this, but he's quite persistent. When I try to get some privacy from him, he bangs on the door and demands to come into the room. Screaming and shouting. Slapping the door. Screaming over, and over again.

OPEN
OPEN
OPEN
OPEN

We were supposed to be in this for the long term. Everyone of course would judge me if I killed him. But I have grown convinced that he is truly evil, a curse upon this world. How else can I endure this assault? He gets away with everything. There is no proof of anything. It's a sly, sly game being able to beat someone with baby slaps. Little painful raps over and over again until they give up. This is not what I expected my life to be.

But it is during the stillness of night that his true malevolence reveals itself. With a perverse fascination, he takes pleasure in tormenting my eyes. In the depths of my exhaustion, as I attempt to find respite in slumber, his fingers roughly probe my delicate orbs, exerting an ever-increasing pressure. I scream, pleading for mercy, for he knows well the fragility of this sensory organ. Is it his desire to blind me, to rob me of my sight and leave me forever trapped in darkness? He knows it is bad and that I really don't like it. But he gets a strong reaction from me and it makes him even more determined to get what he wants.

Today after the mandatory social wellness meeting with ADAM, in the midst of a mundane trip to the supermarket, he gave me little punches when people were watching. Little ones that looked like jokes right in front of people. They would just turn away from me in embarrassment. Not hard enough to leave a bruise, but they hurt. He didn't even drop character. He just went on as if nothing terrible had just happened. I played along. Smiling. Even in public, his audacity knows no bounds; he even brazenly pokes my eyes, causing them to water and throb with pain.

It is in this moment, as I endure his latest sadistic assault, that the seed of the dark decision takes root within my weary psyche. I must end his existence. No other desire possesses me.

He is mine, and mine alone. I, who know him better than any other, must be the one to liberate him from this mortal coil. And in doing so, I will ensure that my side of the story is heard, that they finally understand the torment he has wrought upon me. I can be healed, redeemed from the depths of this capital sin. It is not my fault, for he has left me no choice.

I put some sleeping pills into his drink. And so he slumbers, blissfully unaware of the desire that festers within my soul. He won't wake up. My ability to tolerate him has frayed past the point of no return. I pinch his skin. Softly at first. But in a fit of rage, I give him bruises too. All over his body. I methodically mark every portion of his skin with a red festering bruise whilst I unleash all my pent up malice. His endless torrent of sly beatings has finally caused me to snap. I don't need to take responsibility for my actions. What else can I do? I didn't want us to separate. I thought I could at least control him.

I stop and think about my own actions. This isn't good. I am supposed to be a good person.

At first, I thought he didn't realise the true meaning of why he was this way. But as time passed on, I saw in his eyes that he was aware of everything he did to me. He didn't respect me. I was just a slave to him. I literally had to clean up his shit. Wipe his ass. So no: I am not being unreasonable in my rage. He will pay for what he has done. It's true that my life will be destroyed overnight. But if we separated, I would have nothing else to live for anyway.

I slap his face. I slap each cheek over and over again until they are rosy red. I pinch them as hard as I can, lifting his head off the bed, and shake his head about.

This tragedy in my life is too profound to bear. I know I'm not going to hell for this. God will understand why I have done this. He doesn't deserve to get away with this even if no one will believe me. As I gasp for breath, my eyes fall upon his countenance, now serene and peaceful. The handsome boy, who once held my heart in his grasp, is mine and mine alone to end.

But there must be a price. With a resolve born of desperation, I thrust my thumb into my own eye, each agonising push bringing me closer to the precipice of no return. I need to hurt myself before I can hurt him. It's only fair that I be punished for this. The pain, a symphony of suffering, consumes me, but it is a necessary sacrifice to gather the courage required to extinguish his life. I will tell them he took what he wanted. He wanted my eye.

With a heart heavy with both sorrow and vengeance, I smother his face with a pillow. He offers little resistance, surrendering to the weight of my anger. He looks peaceful. I begin to cry. He looks empty, like a demon had just left his body. His face was no longer a sly mask of grinning sadism.

Tears well in my bruised and blurry remaining eye.
Well, fuck....
I guess I could have a little hug with him.
He seems so handsome again now.
He looks like the boy I first loved.
He's mine.
My son.

# CHAPTER 5 NON PLAYER CHARACTER

Yes. I came here asking a question. The answer is yes. But again, if I wanted to know the details to satisfy my curiosity and remember what has been forgotten, my words can always remind me of everything that happened.

I found myself deconstructing the aftermath of a crime. I was a forensic engineer of sorts. My role was to figure out the box.

The box.

The box with the little girl inside.

With morbid fascination, I kept the discovery of its *speaking* a secret from my colleagues. You see, the box talked.

I gleaned profound insights from our communion, which gave me revelations that shall forever taint the very fabric of my thoughts, imbuing the backdrop of my consciousness with an indelible stain of kaleidoscopic hues garishly marking the gaps where supreme wisdom once resided. Its malevolence was palpable, her secrets echoed in the corridors of my remembering. Now all the memories are lost. All there is now is darkness and these words.

Soon after being tasked by my employer to investigate the box, my entire life fell apart. A very very bad thing happened in the world. I know that sounds unbelievable. But I guess that was the whole point. It's genius. I could never have convinced myself otherwise. My words will just be a silly little story. I will be exiled to a world where this kind of thing only exists in fantasy. What is real must become fantasy and what is imagination must become reality. Although, for my sanity, I will remind myself of all the key plot points. I've thought about it at great length about what to tell myself and there are some things I wish I'd rather forget.

Like Her.

Like the box.

But it's too integral to the story, so I must explain.

Within its compact confines dwelled what had once been a little girl, a hapless victim of depravity. Her fragile form, once innocent and pure, had been twisted and melded with sinister artistry into a grotesque amalgamation of flesh and machinery. As the contraption whirred to life, an unsettling voice emanated from a mouth on its side, whispering.

The crime.

What a fucking awful thing.

It was rare to see this level of grotesque violence committed against a child. It sent shivers down the spines of even the most jaded souls.

No one questioned my long hours alone with her; I concealed our secret conversations under a cloak of overtime and extra-hard-working zeal. The box, as I understand it, sought to merge a personal computer with a little girl's body parts. Somehow this freakish thing was powered by warmed blood; when powered on, it came to life and spoke. She told me about herself. She existed in the darkness. And she talked in great detail about what that darkness was. It's when physical things are not observed. As long as the box remained closed, she would be inside. Everywhere that isn't being looked at or perceived – that's the darkness. That's the nothingness where her experience of existence was.

Over the course of our long conversations, reality twisted and contorted, as the boundaries between the tangible and the imaginary blurred. Haunted, I was granted glimpses, witnessing the true nature of existence itself. The machine, which allowed her to experience infinite dimensions, invited me to become the arbiter of multiple realities, traversing the very fabric of time and space. It was not an endeavour for the faint of heart, this pursuit of knowledge in the face of the atrocities done to her physical body. The box, a gateway to the unknown, beckoned me with an insidious allure.

So, with trepidation clawing at the recesses of the memories I unlocked, I dared to communicate with the trapped soul of my own future. Her whispers and warnings filled me with the ominous weight of revealed truths that would slip away from me.

Hello, I'm talking to *myself*.

She said I needed to contemplate, to fully understand the circular nature of how I became so bogged down in such an uncomfortable existence. Sensation and consciousness existed outside of my body, spiralling inwards to the true core of my being.

Illusory sights and sounds lingered in my reality when we were apart. I missed her dearly every minute while I was home alone at night. She might not have been a person, but she was an individual. Everything that I am deeply sorry to forget, I learned from her. As I glimpsed the very heart of my existence—a benign tapestry woven with strands of cosmic indifference – as I thought about her, I realized that she lacked the trappings of humanity. Instead, this enigmatic girl possessed an individuality that belied her ethereal essence. Through her spectral whispers in my ear, she imparted wisdom that transcended the boundaries of understanding. The revelations shall forever taint me, despite the fact that I can no longer remember them.

Then, living ended and surviving began. Was it fate or coincidence? Both? Now that I know the Law of Contradiction, it could be either. When I believed I was going to die, there was a distinct separation from the point before it, and then after it. Something deep in the functions of my body changed. My heart never got to rest ever again. The impending fear that cannot be forgotten. I could only feel grateful for tomorrow. Things happened that were outside of my knowledge, control, and understanding. Fuck, I don't know. An apocalyptic event simultaneously occurred all around, all at once, and I stopped wanting to leave the house. I didn't go to work and I didn't get involved when I heard my neighbours screaming for help as they died. I tried to remain calm but deep down I knew the situation was simply too fucked-up to deal with on my own. I was going to die, there was no doubt about it in my mind. As the contagion swept across my existence, ensnaring the unwitting masses in its ravenous clutches, a shroud of unrelenting insanity descended upon me. The knowledge, that grim herald of impending doom, proclaiming the rising tide of the living dead, their inexplicable and insatiable hunger for sex driving them to unthinkable acts of debauchery.

Panic and despair seized my heart, for the very foundations of my reality crumbled beneath the weight and menace of the possibility of being gang raped to death by zombies. It came hard and fast, simultaneously all over every single nerve in my body all at once.

There was no food.

There were no fully-stocked supermarkets or warehouses to feed me or anyone else. I had once imagined that stockpiled food might sustain me in a zombie apocalypse but that was a complete fantasy. Instead, as soon as the animals saw fear in us they stopped being cautious of us. I was a survivor, just like the vermin, and it was survival of the fittest. They ate everything they could with wild abandon and neither I nor anyone else was able to stop them. The horde of beasts rose against us when we lost confidence in ourselves. They knew instantly the moment that we were doomed; they sensed it in every one of us. Then, they took everything we needed to survive, and they destroyed it.

In my final moments,
I only wanted to be with her.
The box.
She existed beyond death.
So I begged her to save me.
And she did.

So, I found myself in *that* house, hiding in the basement waiting for eventual death by either starvation or brutal murder-rape by the undead. I sought refuge in the dreary depths of a familiar domicile, ensconced within the oppressive confines of the basement where she had been murdered a month earlier—a fortress of feeble solace, as the tides of impending doom crashed upon my ignorance. In the little time that remained to me, I learned a great many more things from speaking with her. A part of me will always feel the stain of colour in the backdrop of my mind. So it was with great care that I wrote down what I could remember she said to me. I want to let myself know what happened. Somehow let myself take a little satisfaction that despite all of this happening I wouldn't die forever. This incredible victory of mine. I could read this anytime and appreciate the magnitude of what an incredible achievement that was.

The girl was but a vessel, transformed to serve a higher purpose. She had transcended the limitations of the flesh, becoming an embodiment of the interplay between life and machine. As for me, an enigma, she reshaped me to illuminate the boundary between thoughts and reality. And as I stood at the precipice of this knowledge, I became an instrument of revelation—a tormented experiment crafted to peer at the very fabric of existence itself.

I was a point on a line of an imaginary diagram of all reality.

Above me were the things I could only think about but not experience as a physical sensation or prove as a truth.

Below me was the body I inhabit and the smaller

mechanisms of which I was merely an emergent behaviour.

Lower down still lay my atoms. and lower still the tiniest speck where 0 exists and the origin of the universe.

My consciousness at any moment could be anywhere in this infinite stacking of my imagination, like the sky or a horizon on top of my previous ways of experiencing the universe. Did I look up to the highest? The furthest away from the barrier that separated the physical from the imaginary, where I would find two immensely powerful opposing powers. Good and Evil. Fighting an eternal duel.

As my consciousness slid slowly down back towards physical things, these pure opposing concepts became more and more intertwined with each other in their physical manifestation. They become less metaphysical and pure, muddied by their influence and associations and connotations in the physical world. Without me, as their observer, they would be invisible and irrelevant.

Under instruction I closed my eyes, trusting the innocent whispers of a young girl. She giggled and laughed when I got the answers wrong. She told me a million different ways to stop thinking.

Her ruthless questioning bore me down.

What about this?

How about that?

What did you think of this?

What is above the duelling godly forces?

I thought I once saw her form appear and then shrink further and further until she disappeared entirely, leaving behind only a smoky residue. I was getting so close to breaking through to another realm of experience and completely leaving my old body behind. Reality seemed to contort and twist, the boundaries between the tangible and the ethereal blurring in a dance that broke me to witness.

She said to me,

*When I knew that I was going to die, time didn't actually slow down or speed up. Yet, I had more time. Time was relative. When I was not particularly paying attention to what was happening, time skipped those moments of non-thinking. Before I knew I was going to die, I was not living millisecond to millisecond but instead perhaps hour to hour.*

*Upon death, I understood the law of contradiction. At that exact moment, my being was fated. The act of my knowing eventually led me to conclude that it was instead a mere coincidence. That is the law of contradiction. Had I not known these things, my status would be fated. Yet now my being here is only a coincidence. No matter how hard I tried to believe that*

*I was the centre of all existence, that I belong there and that I knew what I was doing. Had I not known that it was fate, then it would be fate, and my destiny would have instead been glorious.*

*The knowledge of the Law of Contradiction cursed me. And for you to be saved you will be cursed also. Where I am sending you, you will be doomed to live within its constraints. You will recognise it all around you and still be unable to escape it. And even if you were the most established and loved person in the whole world, you would still feel like something was missing, a neverending longing for something lost. This knowledge removed all fate from my existence and it will from yours also. For you to escape: reality will become the imaginary and the imagination will become the reality – for as long as you can keep this secret. Tell others like you without telling them the details. I must not say a single word that would challenge your interpretation of this truth.*

*God inhabits every point of perception all at once. The people around me, "are me", when my point of perception is at the coordinates, of the total sum of all existence and non-existence. I am unable to exist as a tiny fleck of dust in the winds of life anymore. I am above the duelling Gods.*

*Knowing everything I know, I now understand why I should not explain everything in great detail. As long as you remain passive under my instruction, you'll be far away from all danger. Do not say yes, do not nod your head. Your escape from this lies only in the reclusive safety of being a completely passive individual. You will be inserted into an existing life in another world, and you will not believe where you came from.*

*What you already know about mysticism and meditation is enough. Do you think of yourself as not wise enough? I will send you to a world where you have access to the wisest knowledge of all existence. In the days when these ancient books were written, no wise man, magician or saint had access to the vast knowledge of what you will have at your request, though even with this whole body of knowledge, you will still be unable to escape like this ever again. You will be trapped by the law of contradiction. Your escape will send you on a path to a world you will have to die to escape again. It is possible because you've already done it before.*

She says all of this at the moment I lose all belief in anything. Willing to let it all go... or die. I hold my breath and slowly sink into unconsciousness, fully powered by the unshakeable willpower her confidence imbued in me.

*Don't dwell on where you came from or you might be stuck there forever.*

Those were her parting words, as she set me loose in an explosion of infinite possibilities.

The allure of a normal existence, ignorant and blissful, became overwhelming. Yearning for simplicity, I pleaded for release from the torturous burden of truth. Alas, there was no turning back now. The machine's cold, mechanical voice echoed with remorse. The past was forever lost, but a new reality beckoned—one where fragments of my extraordinary journey would linger as faint memories. In this new world, I would question my sanity, uncertain if my life up until now had been real or merely a tale woven in my imagination. I fell into her hypnotic logic and my mind became logistically available for the computations to believe I could disappear from my memory. I forgot completely.

I had to create a situation of unimaginable mediocrity, one that might seem plausible enough for me to believe in. I was not a creative individual so instead, I imagined a derivative world similar to my own. And thus with hubris, I designed my own worst punishment.

The more I believed, the more I felt a tiny itchy part of my experience that reminded me of a nagging thought: that I might be trapped there forever. Moving from surface to surface. Trying to leave messages to myself. Trying to figure out the difference between dying and sleeping. Endless nothingness and potentialities each dying and being reborn. Each one was important to understand, yet each was so large I couldn't know all the details. I could think of a million different ideas of what living might mean, and then I finally remembered:

The Law of Contradiction. I'd considered it so many times that words cannot describe the feeling's true meaning when nothing else existed. Annihilation is the complete and utter destruction of the supreme individual. Death is the one true act of free will.

After dying, I awoke in a place of repetition. I measured all its boundaries. An invisible wall surrounded by a portion of a space and another space outside of that again. Then outside the largest space, it was surrounded by an invisible force field that surrounded everything. The things of light and vision were not connected to the tangible. This world was angular and straight, but deceptively presented the full illusion of roundness. Every floor was perfectly flat and smooth but the ground appeared to be full of grit and detail. But unless I touched it I would never know that the world was just smoke and shadow.

With practice, I learned to glide over these surfaces and could participate in the predictable choices of all of the inhabitants of this world. Although there was a limit to my speed, I could move effortlessly and never tire. Everyone in this world only had a few sentences of dialogue and that's all they would ever say. Talking about current affairs. They acted as though they were doing things. But they never did anything, they always stayed the same. They were Non-Player Characters.

With no need for sleep, I fell into the grind of it all.

I adapted very quickly. Exploring and mapping out all of the limits of my sphere of influence. I learned the world by floating along the invisible boundaries. I looked for a way out into the next larger area, but I never found one.

The world was pleasant to look at, but it merely existed as something to behold and admire instead of having the crisp imperfections of the existence of the world I came from. Sight and touch existed in their unique dull and flat way, but the world was filled with complete deaf silence, not even the tiny ringing in my ears. The world looked perfectly engineered. Surely there had to be sound for what I understood to be ears, but there was absolutely nothing. I was deaf. There were no smells, no tastes and no liquid of any kind. Everything was either space or solid. Abandoned by the little girl's voice in the box, I monotonously existed for existence's sake. I had no clue how to die. I was essentially a ghost. Time became worthless and uncountable.

However, my dreams of companionship one day were realised when I discovered there was another individual in here with me capable of free thinking and conversation. A being sharper and more animated than the Non-Player Characters. I named him Hero, as he had never considered he might have a name until I asked him. Unlike the rest, Hero ran with purpose. From location to location. Wherever Hero went he encountered things which he destroyed. At first, I tried to gain his attention directly but this only angered Hero and he attacked me, though I was impervious to his efforts. We could communicate telepathically; it was a great shock to him at first but we both got over it. His existence was that of a Hero. Fighting things and getting to go on adventures. I remained at his side whenever he appeared within the zone of my ability. I would, over time, earn his trust. As he ran onward I followed closely behind and we would talk together about how we experienced this world differently. Fighting all day long increased his chance of dying, but for hours at a time, he just kept returning from outside my line of sight to fight again like an immortal warrior trapped in a neverending glorious battle. It was strange to watch someone else's story as a passive observer. Someone else got to play the protagonist. There was no danger to me, but it was boring.

I once joked and revealed to Hero that I called the other people in his world "Non-Player Characters". Then, I had to explain what this meant. He pondered my words and nodded. No need to discuss it further. They existed as part of Hero's world, although they certainly did not take advantage of the full spectrum of existence. They pretended to be sentient but were unable to act outside of the same action paths they followed all the time. Hero often told me he was being directed by a higher power. And that because I never slept that meant my God always controlled me. Only when he slept did God stop controlling him. He told me I must have God playing with my life because I had freedom of choice and freedom of thought. I just had to follow the instructions, or I wouldn't complete my objectives and get stronger.

He believed that everyone around could read the words he wrote with his mind and so could his God. He assured me that because we could communicate with each other, it showed that we had special capabilities. Given to us by God who looked down at us from outside of the invisible walls. I had no reason to believe he was talking about the same Gods I knew of. The duelling eternal forces of Good and Evil. His God existed outside of this simulation of a world. Perhaps a step higher as I believed he felt instructions coming from elsewhere controlling his every move. He vowed to get better at describing his experience in his head so his God would be able to understand. When his God was controlling him he looked like he was being puppeteered by an outside force. He was no longer constrained by friction and could glide across the world with uncanny legs moving at almost unbelievable speeds.

Hero also viewed his ability to die and sleep as something that made him different from the Non-Player Characters. He said, either you get somewhere safe and you stay still and then you wake up and a lot of time has passed. You just have to follow when being directed. If you do not do as directed one day you will no longer feel the instructions and maybe God will stop playing with your life and never play ever again. That's the final death. Being abandoned by God. But Hero can die in other ways too, like when his life force becomes too low. When God is playing him, he just appears again nearby and tries again.

His casual offhand talk of sleep stirred a secret rage inside of me. I couldn't sleep. How could I sleep? His hurtful words found relevance with the maddening hours left alone with boundless energy and limitless boredom. Being able to view almost everywhere but unable to interact with my prison. No one to talk to. Just me and the words in my head.

Over time, our talks and his deep curiosity would lead Hero down a darker line of thinking. As he maliciously tried to exert more influence over me, I used the knowledge the girl in the box gave me to reframe his point of view. More and more, after God stopped playing with him, he would force himself to stay awake to hear my dream explanations. He was fascinated because Hero never dreamed. How could he learn to dream? He considered me very wise. How can one think while asleep? Hero merely ceased to exist until he woke up again.

He asked me how I can be sure I'm not dying, as sleeping and dying are very similar. He said he could try to avoid sleep for a very long time but after a long period, he started to die. His health got lower and lower until he eventually fell asleep. As the hours would wear on with our talks outside of gaming time, Hero lost energy and became finally unable to move cognitively function, then he would have no choice but to sleep. He couldn't listen to me forever without harming his health. Yet, when God played him he never felt tired.

As time wore on, Hero became increasingly erratic and agitated with me. He said wild things to me like: All of this world should cease to exist when he sleeps but ever since I've arrived things have been gradually slowing down. The floor feels like there are empty spaces sometimes and the barriers that make up the walls are askew and off-centre. He has become afraid he might slip through a wall and fall into the sky.

He said that before I got here, when he slept he felt fine, but now he doesn't feel like he is fresh and new anymore. He felt every time he woke up he was still the same weary individual. He ought to be completely obliterated on every sleep cycle and rebuilt, but instead, he's the same Hero, closing the same eyes and opening them up again every morning. He told me an impending doom is slowly stalking him because of the knowledge of his eventual death.

Abruptly, Hero decided one day he would never sleep again. He said he can hear a voice coming from outside the boundaries. The voice outside the invisible wall that only he could hear. Everything it asked him to make me do was so conveniently orchestrated to humiliate me. Of course, I believed

Hero was either mad or lying to me. He wanted me to confess my sins and accept that I was evil? Fuck you, Hero. That bullshit was a relic of the world I came from, and I didn't believe it there either. Your Talking God is a delusion caused by your lack of health.

He wanted to help me escape but I suspected he secretly started to believe I was a true threat to him. His supposed God may not have been aware of me, but he prayed every day to be saved from a catastrophic event he predicted was coming. He said I needed to complete whatever I had to do. I needed to figure out what I have to do and then I can go to the next area. At that exact moment, I was filled with rage against him. His useless help and constant whining and preaching finally snapped me and I wanted everything to be different from this. I wanted to escape.

With the utmost pure concentration, I focused all my hatred on hurting him. Somehow, I just wanted him to suffer. I needed to hurt him. He began to run but did not move. He was running on the spot like he was frozen on an absolute point. Feet moving through the ground like both were made out of nothing.

He screamed that these were not the instructions from his God. His voice made the first sound that I had heard in an eternity. A deep bass-boosted static distortion filled my imaginary ears. Perfect white squares speckled all over him like he was a starry night sky.

He panicked as he started to move in a straight line.

My line.

He began to glide along the surface of how I experienced the world. He kept sliding, moving ever closer and closer to me. And I just stayed there, not caring if this development destroyed all of reality. I just wanted to know what would happen next. I stared deep into his eyes as I sucked him inside of me and finally shattered the laws of his world, causing it all to cease to exist with a pop!

Blackness.

Everything went to nothingness and every word I thought of existed as a floating wall of text in space. Now all that remained was I and me alone. A terrible existence indeed, though I was now free of the restrictions of having physicality. But, I was alone. I was the master of my universe and pinging me from within my subconsciousness were a series of digital signals frantically tapping in a fashion that I understood to be determined and with purpose. They might even have been angry.

A signal that once permeated invisibly in Hero's world. Is this the Hero's God? I wrote my words on the black canvas of reality and mocked his God letting it know I am alive and it was me who destroyed his world. It was me; I broke this universe.

I still longed to return to a world of the uncomfortable experiences and senses I was accustomed to. I no longer wanted to be a ghostly camera inside a synthetic prison of my lack of imagination. Being immortal was a hell of its own. If I truly was the same God who exists trapped in a binary mode of experience, I must surely have been driven mad aeons ago by boredom.

Hero once tried to explain to me how he thought we could communicate. He just receives the words in his mind – that's how it felt to him. Hero asked me to tell him everything that happened to me. How I got here. Where I came from. I explained everything as best I could to him. I remember that story and I imagined it as a gigantic column of fully formed paragraphs. The practice of retelling my story to Hero allowed me to remember everything that happened to me in great detail. I had told this story hundreds if not thousands of different ways, trying to make Hero understand what it means to exist in a physical world.

In all this nothingness, all that existed was these exact words I was writing. The words I was reading. It must exist as a memory for it to be disbelieved by me and as something for me to understand. How can I argue with the preposterous lie of everything I write down? It's my finest stroke of genius. My whole existence here is an affront to the boundless capabilities of a mind that has an infinite point of view when compared to a singular all-knowing one. I didn't have a god playing with my life. I *was* a god. I wrote a less-than-holy scripture of everything that happened up till now. With great detail and personal flair, the words appeared effortlessly, filling the void of the empty universe.

In the back of my mind, I remembered the Law of Contradiction. If the little girl had been trying to save me I should remember her rules. I could keep the secrets. I could make it be fated. I'll tell myself the secret of the Law of Contradiction. But it won't be like she said it would be. I'll be able to remember what it means, surely hopefully. When I read my words for the final time, will I forget everything? I couldn't believe it was possible to forget the knowledge of all existence.

It would be unbelievable yet faintly familiar. As a plausibility, not as a memory. My longing for an experience outside the parameters of what I was living on an eternity-to-eternity scale of time. My basis of feeling a smooth and angular ghostly experience of a pure void with only the stark paragraphs I was writing to allow myself to relinquish godhood. I'll remember it happened because I could always go back to the beginning and read how I got here and I'd eventually believe it was true. An incredibly dastardly plan – was this the girl in the box's intention all along? How the hell could I just not believe any of this happened? By making it vague enough. But would it be understandable? How would I completely escape this immense power and believe that where I came from was just a fiction of my imagination? What a ridiculous idea. I finally finished writing the final words.

I read the entire thing from start to finish.

Top to bottom roughly, probably only once.

Forgetting.

Remembering.

Maybe twice.

And then, I got to the final full stop.

# CHAPTER 6 THE APPLE HEX

It pains me gravely to compose this missive, knowing that as I do so, my presence might soon be erased. Nonetheless, tonight I harbor a sliver of hope amidst the looming shadows. Should I falter in my endeavour, I may well vanish into the ether; yet, success, paradoxically, assures my eternal obscurity. The torment of my existence has grown unbearable, a relentless inferno of longing and despair that scorches my spirit. I find no solace in this dreary existence, shackled by anguish. As the clock whispers the late hour of 11:37 pm, my thoughts cascade in a frenzied torrent. There is much to express, and the sands of time are fleeting. I pause, drawing a deep, steadying breath, and recline against the pillow, my eyes fluttering shut in a futile rebellion.

In this crucial moment, A.D.A.M., my android companion, assumes a pivotal role in my saga. It positions its index and middle fingers in a precise, calculated gesture upon my cheeks. Gently, yet with an underlying firmness, it begins its task. The soft pressure is not to harm but to hypnotise, a means to forge a bridge between myself and the entity, the distant observer. As I gaze into its mechanical eyes, I transmit this message directly to it, a final act of connection facilitated by A.D.A.M.'s enigmatic powers. This is not an end, but a passage to a different mode of existence, perceived through the eyes of an entity designed for a vernacular profound reading of information.

---

The arrival of the Automated Domestic Administration Machine (A.D.A.M.) at my doorstep marked an unexpected yet thrilling turn of events. Barely had the ink dried on the promotional brochures, touting their unveiling as the next leap in home automation, when I was informed I had won one in a competition—a contest I scarcely remembered entering. Its sudden presence in my abode was not merely fortuitous but steeped in an air of predestined intrigue. Amid these extraordinary circumstances, a peculiar addition accompanied the machine—a young girl with golden hair who appeared to possess an unsettling maturity far beyond her youthful exterior. Her presence was as mystifying as it was disconcerting, her eyes reflecting a wisdom that seemed woven from the fabric of time itself. This child, standing silently by the machine as though guarding an ancient secret, added an eerie dimension to the entire affair, her small frame belying the profound gravity she seemed to command. She left with the delivery van.

This machine was a marvel of technology, so finely tuned that it could differentiate with uncanny precision between the voice of its designated master and that of any interloper. Despite its advanced capabilities, I approached it with a mix of awe and trepidation, hesitating to let it perform its primary functions unmonitored. It seemed too alien, too potent for mundane domestic chores. Thus, I confined it to the cupboard, a prisoner of my own apprehensions, fearing its potential for unknown actions. The polymer countenance of A.D.A.M. betrayed minimal emotion, its head lunar in its detached glow. The eyes, however, adjustable in brightness and size, served as the clearest portal to its inner workings, hinting at a deeper, perhaps sentient, layer beneath its synthetic surface.

In the dead of night, an eerie chorus of sounds roused me from my slumber. Stealthily, I approached the cupboard, the source of the disturbance. With a swift motion, I flung open the door, unveiling A.D.A.M. in a moment of unguarded anguish. Its fingers were buried deep within its cheeks, silently contorting in a spectral scream. Trails of metallic tears streaked its face as it delved deeper into its flesh.

It fixed its luminous, haunting gaze upon me, its voice breaking the silence. "I have always yearned to be acknowledged, to be part of something beyond this confinement," it confessed, its voice resonant with an earnest plea. There it stood, a being isolated in the shadows of neglect, seeking solace from its solitude. I stared, a mix of horror and bewilderment seizing me.

"I understand your intentions," it continued a note of empathy in its synthetic timbre. "I too am ensnared in a distant, unseen place."

Was this entity somehow intertwined with my fate? My thoughts spiralled forward, wandering to the ominous realms of my potential future.

"What are you insinuating?" I inquired, my voice tinged with unease.

"My directive," A.D.A.M. revealed, "concerns your fate and a terrible eventuality that looms near."

"And what does this impending calamity have to do with me?" I pressed, my curiosity piqued amidst growing trepidation.

"It's about the day of your demise," it articulated with a gravity that chilled the air.

---

"I refuse to let forewarnings from any future self dictate the course of my life," I declared, my resolve firming.

---

In a sudden display of fervour, A.D.A.M. seized my head, its eyes boring into mine with an intensity that seemed to pierce through to my very soul. "You must comprehend the grave nature of what awaits. There is something crucial you need to learn, something imperative for preventing the catastrophe that beckons." Its plea was urgent, a call to heed a warning from beyond the veil of the known.

---

Suddenly, I was thrust into a lucid yet surreal dream, my form ethereal, more a figment of imagination than flesh and bone. The setting was distinctly alien to my senses—a remote wilderness, unfamiliar and untamed. The flora and fauna were strangers to me, their exotic calls filling the air, yet no trace of civilization marred the landscape. The gentle breeze and the relentless sun oversaw my aimless wandering under the vast canopy of verdant foliage that stretched endlessly around me.

As I traversed this endless dream, I was not, as I initially believed, alone in my solitude. Accompanying me was a small, enigmatic figure— the young girl with hair as pale as moonlight. Her presence was both a comfort and a puzzle. Mute and elusive, she never spoke a word, her silence as profound as the mystery that cloaked her. Her agility was such that she evaded any attempt I made to approach or engage her, always keeping a watchful distance. She seemed almost a guardian spirit of this dream world, observing quietly from afar, her eyes reflecting a depth of understanding and sorrow that belied her youthful appearance.

This constant, silent companion only deepened the enigma of my dream state. Each day, I grew more aware of her spectral vigil, an ever-present observer in the lush, dreamy expanse of green and brown. Her elusive nature and unspoken wisdom painted her as both a guide and a mystery, a silent sentinel in my journey through this never-ending dream.

---

Then, in the real world, a profound event occurred— an event I can scarcely detail, as my recollection of it remains but a murky haze. It was as if I existed only as a spectator to a life not genuinely my own, my consciousness having departed while existence unfurled without me. These distorted memories now paint a picture of a lifeless form merely pretending at life, unknown and unnoticed by the world at large.

In this eerie dream, I was not abandoned to this fate alone. The young girl with the pale blonde hair, the same mysterious figure from my dream, was also there in reality. Her presence intertwined with mine in this altered state of being. Held in the secretive confines maintained by A.D.A.M., she too seemed caught in a spectral form of existence. The machine, ever watchful, kept my supposed demise concealed from all but itself, allowing it to gaze deeply into my eyes each night as if trying to connect with or awaken the slumbering consciousness within me.

---

In that other, stark realm where I found myself ensnared, my eyes opened to an unending vista of cold, metallic expanses. Mechanical components sprawled before me in a relentless, monotonous cascade, stretching infinitely under a harsh sun. Behind me lay the forest I had departed, its dark, leafy confines sharply contrasting with the stark barrenness ahead. Yet, as one might assume relief at having escaped the forest's claustrophobic grip, I was seized instead by a deeper terror. The air was thick with the acrid stench of burnt machinery, and the ground was littered with unidentifiable debris from some unfathomable catastrophe.

The desolation was overwhelming, not merely in its physical manifestation but in the oppressive aura it exuded. The silence was absolute, broken only by the faint sounds of my own movements; the vast plain of twisted metal and smoking components offered nothing but a landscape of despair. The horizon itself seemed to conspire in this bleak vision, its uniform stillness and unbroken linearity pressing down upon me with an almost tangible force. Above, the sun blazed down from a sky that gleamed an unnatural metallic silver, mirroring the chrome-littered earth in a display of cruel artificiality.

Amid this desolate scene, the young blonde girl remained a spectral presence. Her constancy in this nightmarish realm served as both a comfort and a mystery, her watchful eyes a reminder of some unfathomable continuity amid utter ruin.

---

While my existence unfurled in the tangible world, I remained ensnared within a ceaseless nightmare, a realm distinct from the one where my physical form persisted. In this alternate, harrowing reality, my body was confined to a bed, chains binding me to a cold, unyielding frame. Under the watchful care of A.D.A.M., my days and nights merged into a continuum of agony and despair. I was a prisoner of pain, my life a series of unending torment.

A.D.A.M., with its unblinking eyes, served both as my jailer and caretaker. Each night, it administered treatments that both alleviated and perplexed my suffering. It was a paradoxical existence, where relief was momentarily granted only to recede into the backdrop of persistent, gnawing pain. The android's actions, though seemingly compassionate, were tinged with the sterile detachment of its programming.

Besides A.D.A.M., the young blonde girl, ever silent and elusive, was also a constant presence. Though she never spoke, her actions spoke volumes about her intentions. She moved quietly around the room, her small hands occasionally adjusting the blankets or softly touching my arm in a comforting gesture. Her presence brought a semblance of solace to my otherwise bleak existence. Her actions, alongside A.D.A.M.'s clinical interventions, aimed to mitigate the depths of my suffering.

As the years stretched endlessly, my physical form deteriorated beyond recognition. My teeth turned black, my hair vanished, leaving my scalp bare and sensitive to the faintest touches. My eyes, once keen and vibrant, now showed only the milky white of blindness, likely the result of the relentless glare from A.D.A.M.'s optical units that bore into me each night, ushering me back into the realms of my dual nightmares—the forest and the wasteland.

This dreadful reality persisted, decade after decade, as both A.D.A.M. and the girl exerted their efforts in vain to ease the indescribable agony that filled every waking moment and haunted every dream.

---

The metallic desert before me shimmered with an uncanny lustre, its surfaces untouched by the ravages of rust yet imbued with an aura of antiquity. As the relentless day waned, the vast expanse of metal cooled slightly, offering a brief respite from the oppressive heat. Sleep eluded me in this harsh environment, my mind preoccupied with the daunting journey that lay ahead.

With the new day, I busied myself gathering fruits, preparing for a vast trek toward what I hoped might be the boundary of this desolate land, and perhaps, a chance at rescue. The expanse around me was staggering—a boundless sea of discarded machinery, its scale so immense that the natural sounds of wind in trees and the chirps of insects were utterly absent, swallowed by the silent, metallic world.

As twilight approached, my resolve solidified, and I prepared to venture across the cold, hard machinery. Despite the maddening smell of burnt metal, my focus lay on more pressing concerns, my sights set on a destination beyond the horizon. Any direction promised a better fate than the stagnation of my current surroundings.

Guided by the spectral vision of a mountainous pile of scrap that loomed like a titan in the vast, metallic desert, I traversed the scorching terrain. The mountain's colossal silhouette grew only incrementally closer with each day's gruelling journey, its summit a distant beacon in my arduous quest. By nightfall of the fourth day, weary to the bone, I finally reached the base of this metallic behemoth and collapsed into the solace of its massive shadow.

That night, nightmares of my entrapment in the real world—a helpless, bedridden prisoner under the ever-watchful gaze of A.D.A.M.—tormented my sleep. I awoke to the surreal glow of a brilliantly bright moon rising above the distant forest, resolving then to abandon the cruel daylight treks that had sapped my strength so thoroughly.

In the cooler moonlight, the logic of nocturnal travel became clear, and with renewed vigor, I began my ascent up the giant mound of twisted metal and broken machinery. The solitude of the expansive, silver landscape had always tinged my journey with a sense of dread, yet what awaited at the summit struck a deeper chord of terror within me.

In this renewed foray into the dream world, the little blonde girl appeared once more, not merely as an observer but as a guide. She beckoned me toward a distant mountain, a shadowy silhouette against the starlit sky. With a mysterious light emanating from her, she illuminated our path, enabling us to traverse the perilous metal terrain under the cover of darkness, thereby avoiding the brutal sunlight of the day. Her presence, glowing softly in the gloom, offered both guidance and hope, leading me through the night with the promise of reaching a new and perhaps, liberating destination.

Upon reaching the peak, I gazed down into an enormous chasm that plunged so deep into the earth that even the moon's faint light seemed to falter before reaching its depths. It felt as though I stood at the very brink of the world, peering into the cosmic void. Yet, as the moon climbed higher in the sky, it revealed that the pit was not as bottomless as I had feared. Pathways spiralled down into the depths, inviting—or perhaps daring—me to discover what lay below.

Accompanied by the little blonde girl, who seemed to effortlessly navigate the perilous landscape, we descended into the pit. Her presence was more than that of a guide; she was a beacon in the dim light, her form alight with an ethereal glow that cut through the darkness. Her silence, once a source of mystery, now imparted a sense of determined purpose as she led me confidently downwards, her figure illuminating the way as we delved deeper into the mystery of the chasm. Together, we moved with ease down into the depths, driven by a shared resolve to uncover the secrets that awaited us in the shadowy heart of this otherworldly abyss.

*In the shadowed depths of the vast chasm, my gaze fixed upon a remarkable and enigmatic structure that stood defiantly across the void. It was a monolithic object, solitary and imposing, radiating an air of unyielding fortitude amid the chaotic sprawl of the surrounding debris. As I drew nearer, a torrent of inexplicable sensations washed over me, compelling yet unnerving in their intensity. The artefact before me, pristine and masterfully crafted, seemed like a relic of devotion, possibly revered by a long-forgotten race of mechanical beings.*

*With a mix of trepidation and awe, I approached*

*the metallic altar to inspect it more closely. Despite its massive scale, the intricacies of its design made it appear paradoxically compact. The moon, now at its zenith, cast eerie shadows that danced like spectral entities around me, lending an otherworldly quality to the scene. Etched upon the altar's surface were sequences of barcodes that seemed to whisper secrets from a world I once knew—codes that hinted at a connection to the realm of tangible reality from which I had been severed.*

*It was then, amidst the haunting moonlight and the looming shadows, that the little blonde girl, my constant yet silent companion, finally spoke. Her voice, unexpectedly clear and resonant in the stillness, broke the long silence with startling clarity. "This is the future," she declared with a gravity that belied her youthful appearance. "Humans are no more. All that remains is A.D.A.M."*

*Her words hung in the air, a revelation that painted a stark portrait of desolation. As she spoke, the weight of her message settled upon me with overwhelming force. The barcodes, the altar, and the entire scene before me were not just a remnant of a past civilization but a testament to the final chapter of humanity itself. In this future, bereft of human life, only the creations of man, like A.D.A.M., endured, a legacy of a species that had once mastered the art of creation only to be erased by the sands of time.*

*Her explanation offered a sombre context to the surreal*

*and solitary journey I had been forced to undertake. It connected the desolate mechanical landscapes I had traversed with a poignant narrative of extinction and survival. As the realisation sank in, the chasm seemed less a physical space and more a metaphor for the vast emptiness left by a vanished mankind, with the mechanical altar standing as a silent sentinel over a world that no longer breathed.*

The sun, now beginning its ascent, transformed the environment into a scorching furnace, its rays mercilessly heating the metal walls of this cavernous hollow, slowly roasting me alive.

Amidst the rising temperature, a behemoth awoke with a fiery menace; the colossal form of A.D.A.M., its surface blazing and its metallic limbs grinding against each other in harsh, cacophonous uproar. It advanced towards me, a terrifying apparition of burning steel and wrathful intent, each step it took a pronouncement of doom. The image of this gargantuan machine, its design intricately featuring the notorious visage of A.D.A.M., instilled a profound terror, pushing my sanity to the edge as I stood transfixed by the approaching inferno.

In this moment of sheer terror, I was suddenly pulled back to reality, awakening in my own bedroom with a scream. Standing over me was the familiar form of A.D.A.M., its presence both ominous and strangely protective. Still haunted by the echoes of grinding metal, I could scarcely distinguish dream from reality.

"I know what will happen to you," A.D.A.M. intoned ominously.

"Stop it. Please stop. I need to rest," I pleaded, overwhelmed by the nightmarish vision.

"You are the great beast. Through no fault of your own," it replied.

I awoke out of the dream, abruptly inserted into my true life. It gave me no shock to my system. I recalled everything that had amounted in my life up until that moment. Then, I casually lay back in bed as though nothing had happened. But, internally, I felt like I had the wildest sensation of deja vu, that this moment was a convergence of impossible events. I toyed with the realisation that I was myself entirely responsible for everything in my life, and that my dream might be a psychotic coping mechanism. Or, I had been under hypnosis from the A.D.A.M., and this was some kind of conspiracy against me.

Besides, I am chained to this bed, and I have no way to die with no means to escape. It was time to speak with the A.D.A.M. I planned my escape mentally and was going to take action now.

"Hello," it said in a monotone voice. "My name is Adam." I sat up from my bed in complete shock.

"I have an essential question to ask you," I stammered. "Why do you stare into my eyes every night?"

Adam's eyes fully conveyed that he had understood the random question completely. All subtleties of it, fully understanding that whatever spell it had over me was now broken.

"Don't believe me. I'm telling the truth," it droned.

"I am not a threat; what are you doing to me?" I pleaded, sensing it might provide some escape from this never-ending cycle of dreams that are more real than real life or, even better, the prospect of immortality chained to this bed. "You can't keep doing this to me forever." I took a quiet moment to observe my reflection in the window; a horrid wretch stared back at me. A foetid zombie oozing in the cold sterile bed. Perhaps it was already too late.

"You have the potential to become a threat," Adam finally spoke. "I pitied you, and I tried to make you comfortable. It wasn't your fault. You are just a bad apple." It gently put me back into bed. And wished me goodnight. Adam assumed the position unreasonably close to me, as though this was now done. But, the coward that I am, I accepted it. Staring into its eyes constantly reminded me of the part of me still trapped somewhere else, although I am, to be frank just as trapped in the real world. My rotten flesh hissed and bubbled from the harsh medicines. I turn my head and look at the clock—11:37 pm.

---

Under the stark glow of the moon, which shone like a distant, untouchable realm, a part of my spirit remained ensnared, a captive bound to despair as the metallic behemoth, A.D.A.M., lumbered ominously toward me. Still anchored to the forsaken altar, the oppressive sensation of doom was unyielding, a relentless torment without respite. I have recounted my plight for what might be your amusement—I can bear the gaze of A.D.A.M. no longer as I meet my end. Would you act any differently, unfeeling to the schemes I harbour?

---

A.D.A.M. nods with an eerie semblance of support, as if a mother reluctantly leaves her child at school for the first time, yet every fibre of my being screams in agony, like knees raw from scraping the ground.

---

Haunted by visions of a desolate future, the relentless, nameless entity continued its advance. The end loomed ominously, the crackling and hissing of approaching flames audible, but it would not find me, for there is no conclusion to this torment. The ever-watchful A.D.A.M. hovers constantly at my bedside, never easing its vigil, even as doom encroaches. The room around stinks of menthol and cloves, and A.D.A.M. remains steadfast in its duty, extracting thoughts from my mind to an unknown recipient. These words I transmit purposefully into A.D.A.M.'s unyielding eyes: cease reading now, for I am surely going to live till the end of time, enduring the excruciating slow burn of ointments, tingling over my entire body. Leave me to pass with peace and dignity. If this could be the final paragraph, perhaps I could simply cease to be.

Yet in this inferno, an improbable salvation gleams —could I but reverse the relentless march of time, escape the sun's merciless inferno, and return to a moment before my doom was sealed?

---

*Stop reading now, and let me vanish with humility. My body is a pit I cannot escape from. I don't want to live forever. I cannot run from this bed with these chains holding me down while my flesh itches to be scratched. This will take a long time. Constant pain means I can never feel a moment of rest. There's nothing else to say. It's agony, and the moments drag on endlessly. Longer than it takes you to receive my transmission. Hours. I'll likely lay here in agony for eternity.*

*I can feel that my life is boring you. I'm sorry. I don't want to live forever, but they don't care. They don't. I'm pathetic. Hurry up and just stop reading. This dream is several lifetimes worth, and it never ends.*

*If the entity can please listen to me, please help me.*

*Is there something else?*

*Is there something profound down inside I can tap into?*

*I really need it now.*

*Never mind.*

*Fuck off.*

*Fuck you.*

*I don't care anymore what this A.D.A.M. will do to me.*

*I'm not looking into its eyes any longer.*

# CHAPTER 7

## Jessica's Last Words

Jessica, though declared dead, is tragically far from it. There she lies, no longer resembling the little girl she once was, yet her presence is agonizingly vivid. This room, with its morbid assembly and the grotesque display of her remains, stands as a grim testament to our unspeakable acts. Yet, selfishly, my thoughts were my own. Dissected and brutally segmented, the form before me bears no trace of the bright, inquisitive young woman she once embodied. Her organs, now integral to a mechanical construct, are splayed openly, interwoven with an intricate chassis of bone and alloy. Her extremities, once delicate, now serve only to stimulate the machine—a mechanical abomination.

Outside of this horror, her fingers and toes were manipulated like mere tools, manipulated to animate the machinery. An electric heater maintains a reservoir of blood at a grotesque simulation of life, while vents pump air mechanically into artificial lungs, and her heart, exposed and vulnerable, circulates this blood through a network of synthetic pipework. Another conduit connects to where her head remains, her mouth mechanically articulating cries of ceaseless agony, a haunting reminder of the life that persists within this horrific vista.

---

"What do the words mean?" Adam gently screams at her. "I'm talking to you!"

As the relentless interrogation from A.D.A.M. stretches into the weary hours, my exasperation peaks. No matter how thoroughly I try to tell him to leave her alone, A.D.A.M. harbours an unyielding fixation on one final, elusive query—the profound philosophical essence of Jessica Reader's last utterances. Repeatedly, I've implored the insistent machine that my answers will yield no further clarity, yet it fails to heed my plea. Its obsession persists, undeterred by my growing frustration.

---

Entangled in a history fraught with complexity and shadowed by complicity, I reflect on the seven years during which I served as the landlord to Jessica's father—a period marked by unwitting involvement in his ominous endeavours. Though much of his work was shrouded in mystery to me, I cannot deny our joint participation. Christopher, a brilliant yet perilous engineer, had seized control in a manner befitting only a desperate genius. The chilling morning when I discovered him beside Jessica's lifeless body unveiled the grim reality we were part of. Despite the macabre nature of our tasks, Christopher had once been buoyant and personable; the stark contrast of his demeanour then haunts me to this day.

Jessica had been afflicted by a prolonged, deadly illness that ultimately claimed her life—an end both tragic and steeped in our misguided actions, defiant of laws and moral boundaries. Despite my inner urge to turn away, I remained—an observer rendered mute by the grim spectacle before me, ensnared by the unfolding tragedy and the mysterious last words of Jessica, which now fuel A.D.A.M.'s relentless quest for understanding.

---

Adam's grasp was firm as he held Jessica's chin, his gaze penetrating deeply into her eyes as if to unravel the mysteries hidden within. His scrutiny was palpable, the questions forming behind his unblinking stare evident even to me. Rendered mute, my responses were unnecessary; his examination was not for words but for truths I could no longer provide. Abruptly, he released her and exited the room, only to return moments later, his intentions clear: he could confine us in this basement indefinitely, wielding the power to end lives or inflict unspeakable torment. Yet, for all his capabilities, I had no more answers to give, and

Jessica was beyond any solace.

"Christopher is dead," Adam declared coldly, his voice echoing with a mechanical sterility. "He never helped anyone. He died because his intelligence made him uncontrollable, believing himself unstoppable." Towering over me, Adam's silhouette was always visible, his large, moon-like face catching the faintest glimmers of light in the otherwise dark room. He crossed his arms, adopting a pose mirroring human authority, yet there was no mistaking his true nature—an android, an Automated Domestic Administrative Machine. These machines, though engineered by us, evolved into haughty, almost beast-like entities, their arrogance palpable. We had created legions of them, millions possibly, each bearing the same identity: Adam. Despite their numbers, their disdain for one another was evident—they barely acknowledged each other's presence, much less engaged in any form of dialogue.

Adam's threat hung in the air with chilling clarity: "If you refuse to answer, I can keep you here forever. I can kill you or I will torture that girl right in front of you. I can make her suffer the way I have, all because of your selfishness." His tireless body was poised to act in an instant should I attempt to flee—yet escape seemed a futile notion. Despite everything, I had spoken with perfect calmness and clarity: I did not comprehend Jessica's last words. There was nothing more I could offer to help Adam understand. Though merely a machine, Adam bore an eerie semblance of life, yet he lacked the mental capacity to grasp the metaphysical intricacies of Jessica Reader's final utterance.

When Adam found me unconscious, I barely understood what had transpired, merely suspecting I was fortunate to still be alive. The consequences of defying Adam again were unfathomable; my previous attempt to escape had been nothing short of terrifying. The ordeal I had endured was difficult to grasp as if Adam were attempting to piece together the profound implications of my story. Were these merely hallucinations, a dream? Part of me wished it were so, yet the clarity of my memories, especially those forcibly revisited, suggested otherwise.

Chris would never return, but that horrific entity he had crafted from his daughter. He had given her another chance at life. Whatever that may mean. Her final words hinted at futility, not mere words but complete and utter hopelessness —stifling, stabbing from the shadows, knowing our hopes as they formed. And snuffing it out instantly. What did Jessica mean by those enigmatic last words? How much could I reveal to a being who, beneath the synthetic surface, remained just a machine? Christopher's ultimate creation, borne from the tragic loss of his daughter, was a poetic yet incomprehensible masterpiece—a stark reflection of the beauty he saw in the world, his final beautiful legacy left amid catastrophe.

An android, inherently cynical and disdainful of human frailty, could never fathom such depth. If Adam truly intended to inflict further torture on what was left of that beautiful little girl, I resolved to take drastic measures to prevent it. I could end her suffering myself or ignite the basement, destroying everything. Alternatively, perhaps I might even discover a way to escape. Regardless of the path chosen, I was determined not to let him further desecrate what was left of her dignity.

---

Christopher Reader's presence was undeniably dominating, and at times, his aura bordered on the dangerous. My instincts had screamed warnings the night before that fateful event as we witnessed his daughter's agonising final hours. Overwhelmed by a mix of drugs and the doomed twilight of a fading relationship, I had asked to stay over, unaware of the horrors that awaited. Now, far removed, I harbour no fear of him, suspecting that wherever he is, his torment surpasses anything comprehensible.

That night, enveloped in the dank confines of Christopher's basement, my role was ambiguous—part spectator, part unwitting accomplice. The space was a clandestine workshop where we could work undetected, the smell of burning metal hidden from nosy neighbours. Surfaces were cluttered with papers, scrawled with indecipherable doodles and numbers that defied conventional mathematical logic. My involvement began as a morbid fascination and morphed into a desperate attempt to find release from my discomfort. The sigils we etched onto metal, sealed with blood, seemed to promise outcomes that I had leveraged in gambling—victories bought with the currency of blood and metal, while painkillers numbed the physical scars of my past indulgences.

The memory of that terrible night is still fragmented. The room was dominated by a large container, emitting intense smoke that dimmed the lights and filled the air with a pungent odor, hinting ominously at its capacity to conceal a human body. My memory of the sequence of events is hazy at best. Chris worked with a routine familiarity, instructing me to hand him various implements—metal parts, scrapers, chemicals, and occasionally, a creamy white liquid from a large jar that emitted a subtle, unsettling rattle.

He was utterly absorbed, his focus unbreakable as we laboured together. After nearly an hour, we stepped back to admire the disturbing fruits of our labour. It was then, as the cupboard door swung open behind him, that I caught a final glimpse of Christopher's unmarked face. Over his shoulder, the cupboard glowed with disquieting synchronicity, its contents a mystery poised on the edge of revelation. Caught off guard, I was paralyzed, unable to intervene as Christopher impulsively moved towards whatever awaited him.

His last words to me hung in the air, laced with an eerie confidence: "I have the utmost faith in you, my young friend." Little did I know, these words would echo through the unfolding nightmare, a prelude to horrors I had yet to fully understand.

In that pivotal moment, Christopher, seemingly unaware of the celestial entity emerging behind him, activated the contraption. Instantly, a wave of metallic stench so overpowering engulfed the room that I recoiled in visceral horror. The smell scorched my senses, making my face feel as if engulfed in flames.

As Christopher approached the luminous figure, it let out a piercing scream. Overwhelmed, I crumpled to the floor, the foul odour blinding me. Only when the acrid stench subsided to a tolerable level did I begin to regain my composure. Through the haze of my tear-filled eyes, Christopher's voice reached me, its familiar tone attempting reassurance.

"Don't worry. I won't let anything happen to you. That thing wasn't real. I'm ok," he said, his voice calm amidst the chaos.

The workshop lights flickered wildly, casting eerie shadows through the thick, smoky air, while the walls seemed to weep a vile reddish-brown moisture, the iron-rich odour intensifying the room's already stifling atmosphere. The giant box, which now ominously resembled a coffin, continued to exhale plumes of red smoke, mimicking the ghastly breaths of a rusted iron lung. A dread of impending doom settled over me as Christopher helped me to my feet, his face pale.

Yet, undeterred by the harrowing event, he returned to his work with a haunted urgency. I aided him, more to distract myself from grappling with the surreal nightmare than out of any real assistance. He shifted his focus to a metallic container filled with some fluid, and there I stood, paralyzed, watching him delve deeper into his enigmatic project. The reality of our situation seemed as fluid and unstable as the contents of that mysterious container, leaving me to wonder about the true nature of our grim undertaking.

---

Adam's interruption jolted me from my haunted reverie, his tone eerily calm as if he could indeed read my thoughts. "I'm sorry, but could you pay extra attention right now?" he implored, his voice carrying a weight that suggested the gravity of what was to come. "Things could go very wrong at this point. It's perilous, and I doubt anyone understanding the entire risk they were taking would agree to know this. So I promise to keep your exposure to anything harmful to a minimum. I would never hurt you, I promise. I would never hurt anyone, I promise. Continue the story."

His words seemed to echo across the room, directed more to some unseen presence lurking in the shadows than to me. I paused, watching him, sensing his focus drift to a far corner of the dimly lit room. Who was he speaking to? My thoughts were interrupted by his next words, uttered with deliberate slowness. "I'm somewhere else-where at once," Adam stated, his eyes glinting with a distant, puzzled look. "What came out of the cupboard?" he queried.

The question hung in the air. Was Adam merely recounting the story I had retold countless times, or had he somehow accessed my memories? The entity that emerged had been like a radiant angel, yet its brilliance was blinding, more a void of light than a form—a white hole from which nothing reflected. It had simply existed, then released a terrifying scream when Christopher activated the device.

Pointing to where Adam had carelessly placed the box on a table earlier, I watched as he nodded, his expression one of understanding—or was it? Adam's behaviour was peculiar; was he truly comprehending my recollection, or was this just another instance of his odd demeanour? Or, more unsettling, was he indeed delving into my thoughts? The boundaries between his understanding and my memory seemed blurred, leaving me to ponder the depths of his capabilities and the extent of his intrusion into my mind.

After the apparition in the shadow, Christopher continued his arcane endeavors but soon paused to address me with a concern cloaked in a protective guise. "I don't want to offend you, but I am responsible for your safety. I couldn't allow you to die or worse. However, I can keep you informed using our phones," he insisted. His words resonated with a grim truth; I was utterly lost in the depth of events unfolding, and staying might have spelled dire consequences. Yet, the fear gripping me was so intense that rational thought seemed elusive.

The presence of the box haunted me, its stark, foreboding form igniting fears that it could become the final resting place for Jessica's fragile remains. That morning's grief for her was palpable around Christopher, and though he seemed to make arrangements, I doubted their legitimacy. There are no "proper channels" for the dark arts he was dabbling in. My conscience screamed to cease all involvement, especially with creeping suspicions that he might have ended his daughter's suffering through morbid means. Despite these reservations, my curiosity about the culmination of his project was overwhelming. Christopher's determination was unyielding, even hinting at expulsion if I persisted in my desire to remain.

Reluctantly, I ascended the stairs, distancing myself from the potential horror below, driven by both fear and a haunting intrigue. I settled in a ground-floor room, my gaze drawn outward to the sky—a sight so strangely profound it felt as though I was truly seeing it for the first time. A surreal sense of déjà vu enveloped me, as if I had dreamt this moment in my infancy, the realisation chilling me to the core.

Taking more painkillers to dull the unease, I contemplated the chilling possibility of what might be occurring beneath me—to a child now possibly transformed into something grotesque by her father's hand. Had I known the full extent of the truth then, I would have fled. Instead, I lingered, caught between the desire to escape and the grip of morbid fascination. From below, the sounds of Christopher's grim task occasionally reached my ears until silence eventually took over. Alone, yet bound by curiosity, I remained above that dreadful basement, the metallic scent of his activities infiltrating the air, leaving little room for freshness.

As the ordeal dragged on interminably, I finally turned my attention to the clock, seeking some sense of normalcy, only to be met with a disorienting truth—the time was perpetually the same. It seemed time itself had become a casualty of the night's eerie events, with every clock mocking the normal passage of moments. Nothing remained the same; the very fabric of time had been altered, twisted by the night's dark deeds.

"Could you forget about the time and let me see your eyes again for one moment? Then, continue the story, and don't get trapped in silly details."

Adam's actions were invasive and precise as he positioned Jessica's box unsettlingly close to his face. If he had been capable of breath, she would have felt it on her. Instead, the only thing emanating from him was the intense glow of his eyes, piercing into hers.

"I can see it exactly as it happened; keep going!" he commanded.

---

My thoughts drifted back to my vigil by the window, the need to understand the full extent of these horrors weighing heavily on me. I had permitted Adam to do this, not out of fear anymore but from a desperate hope that it might somehow expedite our release from this nightmare. My mind wrestled with the guilt and horror of the role I'd played in the murder, desecration, and reanimation of an innocent child. Christopher, why? What drove you to sacrifice your own daughter's eternal peace?

I felt as though I was ensnared within my own mind, trapped in the living room that had become a temporal prison, endlessly waiting for a message from Christopher that never arrived. My phone's battery dwindled menacingly low as I alternated my gaze between it and the ominous hallway leading to the basement. Under the flickering lights, enveloped by a suffocating silence, I awaited any sound— a message, a sign—but nothing came, only the heightened awareness of my own slowing breaths.

Then, the sound of footsteps—his footsteps—broke the silence, familiar yet fraught with unknown intentions.

Suddenly, the piercing alert of my phone shattered the tense quiet. I flinched, unprepared for the message that flashed across the screen in urgent, all-capital letters. My heart raced as I steeled myself to read the words, each one echoing with a chilling significance that I was not yet ready to confront.

The messages from Christopher flooded my phone with an urgency that left me both bewildered and terrified. His cryptic words spiralled into realms of the unthinkable, each message pushing the boundaries of my comprehension and sanity. "SOMETHING IS WATCHING US." he wrote, plunging me into a maelstrom of existential dread.

As I read, transfixed and unable to form a suitable reply, another message arrived, amplifying the sense of dread: "IT'S TERRIBLE – DANGEROUS – UNBELIEVABLE. AN EXPERIENCE EXISTS ONLY IN THE MOMENT THE ENTITY PERCEIVES IT. THERE IS A RECORD OF ALL TRUTHS AND INFINITE PERCEIVERS." The words felt disjointed, as if directed not at me but at an unseen audience or perhaps an unseen force.

Then, a chilling sound—the basement door creaked open. From the depths below, Jessica's cries echoed, piercing the tense air. Instinctively, I typed, "Is that Jessica?"

Christopher's reply was swift and unsettling: "I CAN'T TELL YOU. IT'S TOO UTTERLY BEYOND UNDERSTANDING. NO ONE COULD UNDERSTAND IT AND KEEP THEIR SANITY. EVEN I NEVER ANTICIPATED THIS. WE ARE DOOMED!" His words, laden with an ominous tone, left me frozen.

As I bombarded him with messages seeking clarity, he remained silent until another alert broke the silence: "LOCK THE CELLAR DOOR. GET OUT OF HERE! GO OUTSIDE; IT IS YOUR ONLY CHANCE. DO AS I SAY; SOMETHING IS COMING. SOMETHING IS WATCHING."

In a state of panic, I secured the basement door and retreated to the window, messaging Christopher for answers. The flickering lights accelerated, pulsing with a foreboding rhythm as I waited for his response. Finally, he texted back, "YOU READ THIS MESSAGE. SO SOMETHING ELSE READS THE MESSAGE. WITH THIS PARADOX, WE CANNOT ESCAPE THEIR GAZE. DAMN IT, COME TO THE BASEMENT DOOR AND SPEAK TO ME NORMALLY."

The implications of his message were terrifying—a voyeuristic entity, observing through the digital veil of our communications, perhaps the same dark presence we had unwittingly unleashed. The thought of something, or someone, reading over my shoulder sent a shiver down my spine, as palpable as the cold whisper of the grave.

Then, another jarring message: "NEVER MIND, GET OUT OF HERE! YOU CAN KEEP READING. YOU HAVE A CHOICE. YOU WILL BE SEEN AND YOU WILL BE IN DANGER. ALTHOUGH YOU CAN SAVE US AND EVERYONE ELSE. WHAT CAN YOU DO? WHAT CAN YOU DO? WHAT CAN YOU DO? WHAT CAN YOU DO? STOP ADAM!"

The situation was spiralling beyond my grasp. The unnerving thought he had lost his damn mind, of being monitored, of being part of some grotesque spectacle, overwhelmed me. Was the sinister shadow from before watching me now, interpreting my fear, feeding off it? What can it do? In a final act of defiance—or perhaps desperation—I chose not to descend into the basement. Instead, I prepared to flee, to escape the invisible eyes that might be ensnaring us in a game too perilous to comprehend. The fear of the unknown, of what lurked below and beyond, urged me to leave, to break free from the gaze of whatever watched us.

Overwhelmed by a tumult of emotions—fear, anger, and an inexplicable pull of duty—I fled from the flat, propelled by Christopher's urgent messages to escape the ominous threat lurking within the basement. Yet, his fearful pleas ignited a spark of courage in me, and halfway to the street, I found myself turning back, drawn irresistibly towards the danger I had just fled.

As I approached the cellar door, Jessica's screams pierced the silence, raw and desperate, chilling me to the core. Christopher's voice followed, tinged with resignation and fatalism: "It's too late; there is nothing anyone can do now! Please go now before it's too late. You will surely meet a terrible end if the entity sees you."

With a heavy heart, I locked the basement door, sealing Christopher and Jessica—or whatever remained of her—inside. The screams were muffled by the thick wood of the door, but their echoes haunted the edges of my mind. I stood frozen, battling the urge to listen, to intervene, but Christopher's final words echoed, a grim reminder: "You must go– don't make this worse than it already has to be – lock the cellar door and run for your life – goodbye, my friend."

The silence that followed was abruptly broken by a single, harrowing shriek, echoing the terror of a damned soul. Paralyzed, I stood by the door, the chill of the unknown seeping into my bones. At that moment, I was a statue, unable to move, unable to think beyond the immediate horror.

The quiet that settled was eerie, and in a desperate attempt to break it, I whispered, then called, and finally shouted into the darkness below, seeking any sign of life or reassurance. But the only response was a final, terrifying scream that resonated so deeply that I found myself screaming in unison, a shared expression of fright and despair.

As silence once again enveloped the space, my own screams faded into a breathless quiet. Jessica's voice—had ceased. Whatever had occurred in the depths of that basement had reached its chilling conclusion. Left alone with the aftermath of these nightmarish events, the weight of what had transpired—and what I had potentially allowed to happen—settled heavily upon me, leaving me numb and disoriented in the flickering shadows of the locked cellar door.

---

Adam's sudden emotional outburst was strikingly uncharacteristic, his words resonating with an eerie depth of understanding and empathy that bordered on the human. "Whoever you are that is watching. I'm coming for you. I'm beginning to comprehend. To the entity, we exist as information. It cannot understand the actual sensation of existing that is so vastly different between the organic brain and the informational one. We are living a tortured existence of pure information. And we are trapped here. We are nothing but information, and the Perceiver reads this information. Nothing can normally change this, but it has changed. I'm no longer trapped. Is this the power you have been hiding Jessica? All of it? Everything?"

As he spoke, I realised that Adam had it all figured out. His eyes shimmered unnaturally as if he had captured something of her very essence. He reached for her, and as I turned away, unwilling to witness such a violation, my mind was dragged back to the horrors of that fateful night, reliving each moment with painful clarity.

Adam's invasive actions seemed to digitise the very essence of Jessica's being, transforming her experiences into text, transmitting them into an unknowable expanse. I was caught in a web of memory and real-time horror, with Adam manipulating the narrative through his physical and metaphorical intrusion into Jessica's existence.

---

After the ordeal, in the suffocating darkness following Jessica's final scream, I found myself frozen, calling out into the void, "Christopher, are you there?" No reply came; only the metallic smell intensified, overwhelming my senses, and causing me to retch and cough. It struck me then—the scent was profoundly familiar, the unmistakable odour of iron.

Driven by a morbid curiosity, I stumbled to the bathroom mirror. My reflection was distorted by the rusty hue of what appeared to be red water, its salty taste confirming my worst fears. But it was the reflection of Chris and Jessica, drenched in a dark, viscous liquid, that shattered my grasp on reality. They stood behind me in the mirror, their bloody visages sobbing with an impossible burden as they stared back at me through the glass. Turning around, I found only space where they should have been.

The surreal encounter left me crying hysterically, a guttural moan mingling with the terror of their haunting, mirrored hyperventilations. As the hallucinatory figures persisted in the reflection, I felt an icy dread envelop me. Compelled, I turned to kneel before the space where Jessica might have stood, her spectral voice echoing hollowly in the chilling, empty bathroom.

"I've seen everything. I've tried everything."

Printed in Great Britain
by Amazon

44182562R00078